"I ain't crazy," declares the narrator of this stunningly original novel, "I'm not." But sanity is always an elusive thing in this tale that carries the reader through a life torn apart by anger, frustration, and disappointment – but held together by an absolute refusal to "give up."

A first grader who can neither read nor sit still. An angry junior high student lashing out at those trying to help. A self-medicating high school athlete. All this leads us to an adult police officer on the streets of The Bronx at the most crime-wracked moment in New York City history.

The Drool Room *may not make you love its complex protagonist, but it will force you to see life through the fascinating eyes of a remarkable character.*

Ira David Socol

The Drool Room

a novel in stories

RIVER
FOYLE
PRESS

also by Ira Socol

A Certain Place of Dreams

Ira David Socol

The Drool Room

a novel in stories

The Drool Room

First Printing by The River Foyle Press October 2007

ISBN-13: 978-0-6151-6544-8

ISBN-10: 0-6151-6544-8

www.riverfoylepress.com

riverfoylepress@gmail.com

Some stories have been previously published digitally in different forms, 1999-2007. *Davenport Park* appeared in *Spilled Ink: Collected Works of the Holland Writers' Workshop* © 2002 Spinner Arts Publications.

RIVER
FOYLE
PRESS

for James –

*"A remarkable tale," I said, as the old man stopped to relight his pipe.
"What happened to the boy?"*

(Chris Van Allsburg, The Wreck of the Zephyr*)*

Climb

This time, climbing the huge tree, I could see only the wide sky that opened above me. My hands and feet still found the branches cleanly and surely. I still heard the calls of the other kids below, awaiting the rain of chestnuts I would hurl down to become everything from baseballs to hand grenades in the outstretched hands; even afternoon snacks once roasted over the trash barrel fire already burning, sending its waves of bent light upwards into the cool autumn evening. But I could feel the world falling away. The tree held the line between the rear of the apartments and the massive stone wall that held back the old schoolyard three stories above, and with each lift of my body the universe widened.

This time I had other places to go. Better places. Different families. I could see an island reached only by boat, hiding beyond the shoreline fog. My father a fisherman who takes me with him most mornings onto the gray Atlantic. A place without schools and worry and failure and hurt. The places I had found hidden on the edges when I was so horribly tired but still could not sleep.

Now the only thing around me is the chill air, and the sounds beneath me, all of them — even the shouts of the kids have faded away. And all I want to do is give up, and fly.

The Tower

The tower rose as a medieval threat above the central doors. The building sat at the edge of the hill where the city plummeted from the high ground of the roads linking New York to Boston to the salt-marsh shores of Long Island Sound. A wide lawn rolled along the Shore Road. If you followed the long sloping drive down from the gates on Centre Avenue you could get in through a gothic tunnel to the basement, or by climbing gigantic stone stairs and passing through cathedral-style doors into the main hall by the auditorium and the principal's office. I spent more time in the auditorium than I did in the principal's office. I spent far more time in the offices of the assistant principals than I did in the auditorium.

The school, a 1920s version of a Norman fortress, was filled with memorable spaces. The auditorium itself, balconied and lined with regal windows hung with green velvet draperies, the gymnasiums like enormous medieval training halls, classrooms defined by vast tall windows and rich oak floors, and the catacomb like spaces below where shop classes were held. But I remember less public rooms best.

Mr. Collins, who was the huge black assistant principal, had a pale green office with dark green curtains and pictures of his high school and college basketball teams. Mr. Schiavone, who was the huge white assistant principal, had a grubby white office with blue curtains and pictures of his wrestling and football teams. Neither had carpeting. Both men were known to be violent. In fact, I suppose though no one in the school system would ever admit to this, they had both been hired to replace the ancient 113-year-old Miss Maroney when she retired soon after my arrival, simply because they could be trusted to be violent enough to scare the increasingly hostile student body.

Two and three floors above the entrance by the auditorium were two huge rooms, one above the other. They must have once been classrooms before fire codes began to be enforced. These rooms occupied the tower on the third floor above the library. They were vast rectangles with four round turret spaces, one on each corner, joined to the rest of the school by a single open staircase with elaborate carved wooden banisters decorated with knights and gargoyles. Our school's sports teams were the Knights, the right choice for a Junior High that looked as this one did. The wrong choice for a somewhat inner-city lower-middle-class-to-poor student population that could barely muster simple social expectations much less chivalry.

In seventh grade I had this gigantic crush on Cindi Lefferts. It was somewhat reciprocated. I think she most liked having a boyfriend her parents hated. With a little more self-respect I might have had a problem with that; but, as it was, I took what I could get.

Cindi loved passing notes back and forth in classes. In English, before I got shifted to the retard class, we kept getting caught. The teacher would read the notes out loud to try to embarrass us. That worked at first, but I got wise. One day my very obviously passed note read, "Mrs. Hairston sucks cock all day." She grabbed it from Cindi's hand and started to read. It isn't easy reading my handwriting and in concentrating on the combination of my strange letter forms and her own rush to make me look stupid, she missed the chance to scan for content. She stood in the middle of the room and read, "Mrs. Hairston sucks cah...," before she realized what she was doing. The class laughed for the rest of the hour. For weeks kids pointed to Mrs. Hairston in the halls and laughed. I was a hero. I was also dumped to an English class where Dr. Suess was heavy reading.

No one really entered the school through the tower doorways, except perhaps when running in from cutting classes. Then maybe you'd use the ground floor route. The main entry to the building was out on Centre Avenue; four huge wooden doors were set into another dramatic gothic arch, centered between the gothic stone screens that defined the windows of the gyms – girls to the north, boys to the south. This was closer to the tiny teachers' parking lot and, obviously, closer to the street where any visitor might park. It was also a long way from the offices and because of the noise from the gyms, not a place where a banging door would be heard. Most kids came in that way in the morning though some of us favored the Church Street driveway at the other end. From there you'd go into the cafeteria on the ground floor of the "new wing." Breakfast was cheap and available until midway through first period. There was coffee too. That was supposed to be for the teachers, but no one cared what you chose to drink.

My admission ticket to regular ed in Junior High was going to see the social worker twice a week. After an incident in English a weekly session with a psychiatrist was added in. The three social workers had offices on the lower of the two tower floors. Not offices really. Each had a desk in a corner turret. In the middle, separated by some primitive predecessor of the open-office partition, were various places to sit and talk. The psychiatrist used half of the floor above; the other half was filled with file cabinets and bookshelves.

The social workers talked to me about "using [my] limited skills wisely." This was really the only topic though the specifics varied. They always opened by asking me if I had any problems "right now." I always took the "right now" quite literally and said "no." This was much like claiming in church that you had nothing to confess. It was frowned on. But while in the church the time I would spend waiting in line in front of the confessional was used to rehearse the right selections of sin, in the tower I would simply resist. Perhaps I was more afraid of God than all the might of the school. Perhaps that was a mistake.

The best place to smoke cigarettes, we thought, was way across the football field from the tower – at the corner where Center Avenue met the Shore Road. A monument stood there, facing perpetually locked iron gates and the street corner, with bronze rows of the names of people who had died in some war. Civil War? Spanish-American War? Now, based on the age of the school building, I'd guess it says "Great War," but there's no evidence in my memory. It was completely shielded from the school side by massive evergreen plantings and the giant stone of the memorial itself. From the street side in fall and spring you'd be shielded by flowering trees and bushes. In the winter the cops would often call the school and bust us. We'd wonder why. We were city kids. That lack of leafy anonymity was a persistent mystery to us.

Once I'd say "no" to "the problems"' question, the social workers would inevitably pull out a folder with papers inside documenting the crimes I'd committed over the past 48, 72, 96, 120 hours. Not all crimes – misdeeds and acts of "bad judgment," or even "questionable judgment" were included. They'd begin with a list, making it clear they considered my "no" a serious lie. The fights, the smoking, the cutting classes, the no homework handed in, the yelling at teachers, things like throwing an eraser at Mr. Clarke, would all be brought to my attention. "Well," they'd say then, "do you really think things are going well?"

This question is a trap. When you're a kid, you're surrounded by traps. It isn't fair; but that's the way it is. Especially if you're in a tower with just one stairway out and are outnumbered by adults. I'd never said, "Things are going well." I'd never said that at all. But adults throw questions at you that force you to lie, or to say that you've lied, which is the same thing – even though their question is a lie, you're the one getting in trouble. So I'd do the only thing I could do, which is shrug the "I don't know" shrug and not say anything because then they've got less on you.

In general, I'd say only what I absolutely had to in these sessions. Words rarely help in childhood or adolescence. You don't have the verbal skills to compete yet. Sometimes silence is smart. But non-responsiveness is not. That gets you sent to really dark places. I'd witnessed that path. Walked along it briefly. Didn't like that result. So I said what I had to – was forced to. Shrugged a lot. Nodded sometimes. Learned that a brief effort at crying once every couple of weeks had the effect of creating probably undeserved, but very welcomed, sympathy – and used it as necessary.

We drank up on the hill behind the tennis courts. Only beer. There were winos with their Mad Dog 20/20, but we looked down on them. Morons. Wine gets you sloppy – beer makes things fun. We smoked pot various places: on the landing of that big outside stone staircase – pressed flat against the wall in the belief that no one could see us. In an unused stairwell that led to a forgotten sub-basement near the gym. On a catwalk high above the auditorium stage. Billy Donatelli and his buddies did smack in the hallway behind the band room, but me and my friends stayed away from that junk back then.

What you say and don't say to mental health professionals is a game and the more I got to play it, the better I got. First, you need to know who you're talking to: Women are usually different from men. Social workers are different from psychologists. Psychiatrists are very different. "School Psychologists," who are not really psychologists at all but maybe glorified guidance counselors have, in my experience, been pretty useless help wise, but you can play them pretty easily to get what you want.

You learn the phrases. You offer contrition without any promise of an attempt to change behaviors: "I have no idea why I do the stuff I do." Sometimes, with male social workers or psychiatrists of either sex, you can add force by saying, "I just don't understand why I do the shit I do." You can shift their focus to issues they are unprepared to deal with and thus buy yourself some time: "If things were just OK at home and I could sleep, I'm sure things would get better." You can get social workers to push you up to the psychiatrist level (or at least psychologist) by suggesting: "Everybody would be a lot happier if I was just dead." This can also buy you time, but can come with many undesirable con-sequences, and becomes disastrous beyond the age of fifteen. Often it's best to ask them questions, which both strokes their egos and takes the focus off you: "Well, I don't know what to do when that happens. What did you do when you were my age?"

In metal shop, in eighth grade, Kevin McCauley made a bong out of aluminum. A truly beautiful thing. This was OK until he started using it by the garage door near the car-lift. That might've still been OK but when Mr. Andrews caught him, Kevin said it was mine. Shop was my success and I didn't like that being threatened. So I got mad. I said, "Mine huh?" I grabbed the bong from Mr. Andrews and hit Kevin over the head with it. I think it was half-bullshit at least, but he acted like he faint-ed and acted like he had a concussion. Thus, it became an actual crime.

The actual crime shifted the focus in the tower. Now I met with the psychiatrist three times a week and checked in with the social workers only for tests and stuff. The more trouble you were in the higher you were kept. Was this true for prisoners in medieval times? I should have asked in History. I did like the view from the top of the tower though. I'd stand waiting for my turn staring out the windows across Long Island Sound. I could see the old fort and the ruins of the beer-garden castle on Glen Island and the lighthouse on Execution Rocks. I could see the soft green hills of Long Island's north shore and if it was clear and I leaned out the window, the towers of Manhattan. So many places for me to run was I not trapped by age and circumstance.

After the actual crime the questions in the tower got more compli-cated. Maybe they should have, though I had a different opinion. Every-body likes police tactics and tough justice when it's applied to somebody else, someone seen as dangerous – but even the most right-wing law-and-order type becomes a liberal the moment a cop pulls him over for speed-ing. In my mind, I was only defending myself. But in the reports, I was "increasingly violent" and "increasingly disruptive" and "showing increases in inappropriate behavior." If you are running an institution based entirely on the concept of compliance, which is what a school is in our society, a student like me is a huge threat in so many ways.

So now, I was expected to agree and make promises. Confess perhaps, then agree, and then make promises. The words have to be changed. The tower seems frighteningly high.

My days were changing. Falling back into the Special Ed pattern of elementary school. Resource rooms and the tower. Tests and analysis. Broken only by avoided classes and sports practices. Football in the fall. Basketball in the winter. Baseball in the spring. I didn't make much of an impact on the football team, though I got to alternate at halfback bringing in the plays. But I mattered to basketball and baseball, as a point guard and a catcher, and those coaches – I suspect – were the adults who fought to keep me more-or-less in school.

I probably went to a few classes. Though if I did I sat in the back and avoided contact with education whenever possible. And it was easy to do this because an uneasy truce was settling in between me and the teachers. They didn't bother me and I didn't bother them. Even when good, wonderful, nice teachers thought they might "get through" to me, thought they could help, I couldn't allow it. My image was all I had left and my image demanded, if not full-time insolence, at least total non-participation.

Drift set in, as it has often tended to do, at least since the structures of the school day were introduced. Not all the time – of course not. There are weeks, months, seasons, once in a while whole years of lucidity and tremendous accomplishment. At least by the scale with which people like me are measured. But those winning streaks alternate with two other time signatures, the crash and the drift. The crash is both self-explanatory and at least has a definite ending of sorts. I'll admit it is not an ending you look forward to; even the most suicidal person, having leaped from a rooftop, must fear the moment when he strikes the pavement no matter how much he seeks what is on the other side. Also, I have always been clearly aware of the crash when I'm in that stage, which makes it different from the drift.

In the drift I am disconnected from most things though not from assault and pain. In fact, in the consciousness vacuum that defines the drift, touches both physical and emotional becomes assaults, and pain is magnified to remarkable proportions. In this drifting time, I wandered the floors of the school chased by everything: The hum of fluorescents attacked, the noise of feet in the corridors struck like hammers to the skull, the smell of old chalk dust choked. The voices of teachers cut into me. The slam of lockers punched me. No amount of ingested alcohol, THC, or nicotine could quell enough of the hurts to allow me any comfort.

So, no matter how much they talked to me up in the tower, no matter what I promised up there with the great view and the ancient softness of old incandescent lights and the insulation of distance from the pain generators two floors below, it could not hold once I was returned to the mainstream. The longer the drift went on the more dangerous I became. This is still true though age has thankfully slid the scale downward. Any touch, any loud verbal direction, was perceived by my damaged brain as a full-scale, life-threatening situation. Fights multiplied, culminating, a little more than a year after the bong incident in what became my escape.

All my adult life I have tried to forgive both those who've tried to help me and those who've tried to love me. The latter is a different tale of regrets. What can you say about people – whatever their motives – who have given it their best but still come face-to-face with my insanity? That I tried to warn all of them. That's all I'll say here. Except my parents and there are different apologies for each of them.

It is harder for those who've tried to help. Resentment stalks these memories, maybe anger. Perhaps because I simply don't understand why they've tried. Perhaps because they tried without studying the situation deeply enough. I know – you see someone in a horrible accident and you run to them and drag them from the car because you've been raised on movies where crashed cars always explode, which isn't true except for certain Pintos and some Chevy Trucks, but how would you know that? And in dragging the victim out of the car you cause serious nerve damage or something. You're still a hero, especially if you've been hurt badly yourself in the rescue, right? So it's not fair for the now twice-wounded victim to be angry with their rescuer, of course not, but it happens. It does. I'm sorry.

Mr. Hamilton was not a bad guy. Not in any way. He taught ninth grade American History to a class filled with wounded and hopeless children who occupied almost adult bodies. What do you do with a room like that? Almost thirty kids, all but three boys – the best of whom were the ones with no chance at all – those with IQs below 80. We knew who they were. We knew all about each other's problems. The worst of whom, like me, were smart enough to be dangerous, frustrated enough to get viciously angry – whose issues seemed to make us hopeless but – well, good people always think that if they could just, then maybe, and things would be different. Mr. Hamilton, I think, was good people.

On a Thursday I got into a fight just before class with Eric Chapel. This was unfair. Eric was bigger than me but way slower, both physically and mentally. I shouldn't've been getting into it with him at all. But I was already more than a year into the drift, probably a bit drunk, and very on edge. He said something like, "You think you're better than me, but you're just another retard." It's always the truth that gets you. This got me and I hit him. I hurt him.

Mr. Hamilton grabbed me. He had to. Then he made a crucial mistake. He made his decisions based on a trust he had in me. Because I actually said something about history once a week. Because if he talked to me one-on-one he could almost get me interested in this subject. Because he was fascinated by my love of maps, especially maps of obscure places and times. Because he thought I had some kind of potential. Because of all of those things, he believed that he could let go of me and reason with me.

There wasn't an immediate reaction. Later, the psychiatrist told me that if my reaction had been immediate many might have been more likely to excuse what happened next. Maybe. I don't know. At first, everybody agrees – I listened. Two witnesses said I was on the verge of tears. Mary Caprone said I was crying. Danny Moradini was the only one I know of who said that if you'd been watching my hands and not my face, "Your face was totally fuckin' blank dude," he'd said, you'd've known exactly what was going to happen.

Mr. Hamilton was hunting for words. He found the wrong ones. He said, "You've just got to try harder." I remember that. So did others. That was the trigger. The worst thing I think you can say. Though even now it is hard to describe why. And I cold-cocked him. One punch. Catching him totally by surprise. A really terrible attack.

Mr. Schiavone was already on his way – he'd heard about the first fight – and was coming to smack me and suspend me. That was the pattern. He'd slap you really hard in public, then grab you by the ear if you were smaller or bend your arm behind your back if you were bigger and walk you to his office. The publicness of it all being the educational element. In his office he'd hit you again. Then he'd call your parent. Then he'd suspend you. Sometimes he'd hit you again once more before you left.

But that was for small stuff. I was way past small stuff. So at that moment, Mr. Schiavone landed his full body on mine driving me in a pro-wrestling move back into the blackboard; the chalk tray cutting into me so deeply the bruise took five months to completely fade. Then he grabbed me, slammed my head against the wall, and punched me – breaking my nose. He never approached Mr. Hamilton. He left that for someone else. Then he bent my right arm behind me and dragged me away, not to his office this time, but up three flights of stairs to the top floor of the tower.

He threw me onto the floor, hard enough that I slid and slammed into the wall. I thought my back was broken and blood was pouring out of my face, down into my mouth and across the obligatory white T-shirt. Still, I could hear. I lay curled into a ball by the wall and listened. Mr. Shiavone blamed all this on, "You bleeding heart shrinks who kept that little brat in the building." He said that if the police weren't called he'd break my head open. I think the psychiatrist looked at me, saw the blood, and took the threat seriously.

The police did come, four of them in all, one a Sergeant. But Mr. Hamilton came up and would not press charges. So the cop could only grab me, lift me up, and bang my head against the wall once more for good measure. "I'll knock some brains into ya," he said and then dropped me back to the floor. Mr. Hamilton tried to talk to me but Mr. Schiavone kept yelling and I had nothing to say. He should've pressed charges. Then I wouldn't've owed him – and I could've forgiven more easily.

They didn't let me back into any "regular" classes. I did the rest of ninth grade in a dark classroom near the art rooms in the basement. Even there you could escape. No one cared. Plus with me they had the threat of Mr. Shiavone. They knew if I went out the window I'd stay out. As far away from the school and his fists as possible.

The only solution, of course, was "Alternative High School" and so I was sent there. A punishment. But I got there after a full summer. After the drift had faded. It was a much smaller school with an open schedule. There were many fewer teachers – most of who thought I had at least "some sort of potential." And that made it all work better than any school since first grade began.

There's something about picking the right background – if you want to be seen in the best possible light.

Davenport Park

You're not allowed to swim at Davenport Park, which is why I swim here. It's no beach full of people I know or don't know. Just me and the cooler, faster waters of the Sound – out where you find the currents.

I come here at night, leave my clothes on the twisting, tumbled rocks, and jump in. My dad told me that glaciers turned these rocks over when they dug the Sound from the earth, but that was so long ago. I swim out to Huguenot Island, only half or three quarters of a mile. If I'm still not tired I swim the mile over to Fort Slocum. I like walking naked on those abandoned streets. I should live there. The harbor patrol would never find me. I'd move into one of the old officer's houses, in my own world, where no one could fuck with me.

A Tour of My School
including the Room that was Supposed to be the Book Room

Part One: When

I had come back to New York for other reasons. It had been many years
– far longer than I could have ever imagined – when I left to go try to do
something new, to be something different. Now those new things had
brought me to a hotel in midtown Manhattan.

I had expected to indulge in only selected memories. I would eat
New York pizza and great Chinese food and have pastrami on rye at a
kosher deli. Someone had hooked me up with tickets to see the Rangers
play at the Garden. I would wander the Metropolitan Museum and go
ride the escalators at Macy's. The plans were made.

But I was close. I guess too close. And I had to go look.

I rented a car, an amazing extravagance in New York, but I had no choice. I drove out of the city, just beyond the border of The Bronx, to my hometown. I started very early and went opposite the rush hour. It was still early when I got to New Rochelle.

I had breakfast at the Thru-way Diner. The building was different but the food and maybe even some of the waitresses were the same. I was about to order lox on a bagel then switched to the fried egg on a roll. That had been my basic meal when I'd cut high school classes and come here in the mornings. We called it "The Breakfast Club" – at least Denny and I did. A fine title to explain our non-availability in school from ten to noon each day. Others were invited on most days, one or two, to fill out a table and conversation. Guests on the truancy express. There might have been a moment when I wondered at the path from then to now – here I was, after all, back in New York for professional reasons with people paying to listen to me – but I let that thought pass. I finished a fourth cup of coffee. Left a tip. Paid the bill. Used the men's room. And pulled out of the lot onto US-1, Main Street

I drove past places I had lived, played, and walked. Past the houses where friends had lived. I saw the high school, the parks on the waterfront, and the remnants of the great movie theaters, one of which now seemed to be a "Wicker Warehouse." I stood in a cold coastal wind and looked at the rocks near a beach where I had hidden one Christmas morning when I didn't want to go home and didn't want to be found. It had been cold then too.

And then I was driving from that place to another when I stopped for a red light and found myself there. I was on the Shore Road, a little east of the corner of Church Street, when I looked to the left.

There stood an unremarkable brick building fronted by a narrow parking lot; the driveway entrance just across the street from where I sat. A thin line of bushes near the sidewalk looked no healthier than they had thirty-five years ago. Candy wrappers and other garbage were still caught among the branches. Above a concrete canopy that sheltered the front doors, big aluminum letters continued to announce "TRINITY SCHOOL" and "CITY OF NEW ROCHELLE." Under the canopy, I saw again the ceramic plaques set into the front wall depicting the evolution of transportation. The squares – one each for ships, trains, cars, and planes – showed an antique form moving left to the east and a modern version, circa 1950 and much larger, moving west. I assumed that the front of the diesel locomotive still had a spot where the glaze had been broken away revealing the rough clay beneath.

I stared until the light had changed and those behind me honked. But I couldn't leave right away. I pulled over and parked. Then I got out and stood facing this place, jacketless in the cold, just like then. First, I remembered five seconds, a fragment of time that played in my head like an old Super-8 movie: the colors faded, the images marked with scratches, the motion slightly jerky. Then I looked again at the street, the driveway, the building, and I realized that there was almost no detail of that school that I could not recall.

Maybe that's a surprising thought but it really shouldn't be. Except for homes in which I have lived, and only some of those, I was in that school building more days than I have been in any other building. I figure it this way. I was there for seven years and I am pretty sure that school years have just about a hundred and eighty days each. I can't do that kind of math in my head – I'd have trouble with this arithmetic even on paper – but a calculator tells me that adds up to one thousand, two hundred and sixty days or almost three and a half full years. I have only lived in three places for at least that long, but I have lived in fifteen places that I can remember in my life. I have only worked in one place more than four years and, of course, I did not go to any place of employment every day.

The one job I had for longer – I spent six years working out of one building – but because of an unusual schedule a work year was only two hundred and twenty-five days. That would add up to one thousand three hundred and fifty. This would be more except that in every year I worked there I had at least twenty-eight vacation days (so I subtract one hundred and sixty-eight) and once I got hurt and was off work for more than five months (so I subtract at least ninety-two more), which means I'm down to one thousand and ninety. But even that is too much. I had other injuries that took days away, and we could take all of our over-time hours in time-and-a-half time, so I had many other days off as well. So just a few over a thousand is my best guess there.

In any case, I do not recall that building – the NYPD's 47th Precinct Station House – nearly as well. Even with all those days worked there, I really didn't work there. I arrived there to start my workday. I put on my uniform in the basement locker room. I picked up my radio car keys and portable radio near the side of the desk. Sometimes I ate lunch or dinner there, down in the room we called our lounge, or I might have worked out in our gym instead of eating. At the end of the day I would shed my uniform, sometimes take a shower, get dressed, and leave. So most of my days were spent in a police car not the building. Even when arrests were made only maybe an hour was "back at the house," as we'd say. The rest of the time, sometimes ten, sometimes twelve, occasionally twenty hours of "processing" was spent at the Criminal Courts Building down by Yankee Stadium. Not the cool, big Court House you can see from Yankee Stadium, that's the Bronx Supreme Court where the big trials are held. The Criminal Courts is down the street a ways, pretty well out of sight.

None of that has anything to do with this story, not really. I just bring it up because I need to explain, at least to myself, why my memory of Trinity School is so strong compared to other places. Unlike the Station House, when I went to school I was pretty much there all day. Even though, sure, there were sick days and snow days which might cut the count down some, I more than made up for that with a bunch of summers spent working for New Rochelle Parks and Recreation running summer recreation programs at the school on the days when I wasn't scheduled to lifeguard, or when it was raining and I'd go down to Trinity and open up the gym so kids could come in and play basketball. This was better than being sent home from the municipal pools and not being paid for the whole day.

The only other way it might connect is this – I don't think anyone who knew me back at Trinity, either when I was there from kindergarten through sixth grade, or when I was working for the Parks Department, would have ever guessed that I would end up as a cop. I think they would have laughed at that thought figuring it far too strange to consider. There were a lot of reasons for that. Still, for two weeks in sixth grade I was on the Safety Patrol. But then those of us on the Safety Patrol got caught smoking and running and yelling in the halls. Those were two separate incidents. There were others. They disbanded the Safety Patrol. Before I entered the New York City Police Academy that was my only police experience, although I had worn mirrored sunglasses for many years.

Maybe I should say this next, because otherwise you might be confused. Trinity School is a public school. Most people, upon hearing the name, assume it to be a Catholic school but it is not. New Rochelle, New York, is a pretty Catholic place, especially the southern half of the city, but that is not where the name comes from either. The fact that it is a public school probably makes a difference. Catholic schools worked differently than public schools, especially back when I was a kid. Most Catholic schoolteachers were nuns in black. There were many Catholic schools I could have gone to: Blessed Sacrament and St. Joseph's, just to name two, but my family was not big on church stuff. And there were public schools in New Rochelle that seemed like Catholic schools. At Jefferson and Columbus and Stephenson, boys had to wear white shirts and ties on "Assembly Days" and all the kids had to stand up when the principal walked into the room. But those schools were all in deep Italian neighborhoods: the South-Side, the East End, the West End. Trinity's neighborhood was the South End and the downtown. It was a mixed place: Irish, Italians, Germans, Jews, even the rich kids who lived along the shore of Long Island Sound and who had liberal parents who believed in public education. Of the schools in this end of town, Trinity was the one where they might do things differently, where they might try things out.

If you went in through the school's front doors, which you weren't really allowed to do as a student, the office would be ahead of you, just to the right, hidden behind frosted floor-to-ceiling glass. There was a big solid wood door to the Principal's office ahead and to the left, both offices sitting across the main corridor. To your left, just beyond the entry, were the two sets of double doors that led into the auditorium. It could hold almost the whole school in its theater-style seats along the long floor that slanted down towards the stage; it must have seated close to a thousand.

That may seem like a lot to you. I have since discovered that once you move away from New York City elementary schools are much smaller. Even Trinity now has far fewer students, which makes it strange that they've made the building bigger, though I surely wouldn't object. But back then, I just assumed every school was that big. We had five or six classes to a grade, thirty or thirty-one kids to a class, with seven grades. I always want to say six grades but then I remember you have to count kindergarten. So seven. It was a big school. I'm not sure how much difference that fact makes.

The gym was on the other side of the entrance hall from the auditorium but you had to go around the corner to get to it. It was a pretty good basketball court for an elementary school. It had mats for tumbling and ropes for climbing. Across the hall from the gym was the nurse's office. When kids wanted to get out of gym, especially when it was a "climb the ropes" day, they played sick and went there.

There were only two other things on that main hall which formed the base of a U-shaped building. Across from the auditorium was the "GP Room" – "General Purpose" – another auditorium, much smaller but still equipped with theater seats and a slanting floor. Here we watched many, many, movies. Further down was the music room. Off the GP Room was the AV closet and AV room. Sometimes, when teachers decided that their classes ran better when I was out of the room, they let me rewind movies and set up projectors there. This had an extra-benefit from their point of view. The principal's office was right next to the AV room; he even had a back door that connected to it – I was thus super-vised.

Teachers decided that their classes ran better when I was out of the room because I have what is now called Attention Deficit-Hyperactivity Disorder, although I think this is a bad name for what is meant by it. But when I was at Trinity School they didn't have that name yet; they used the term "hyperkinesis" instead. The words I remember most were less clinical. Teachers first said I was "restless" or that I "had a hard time sitting still." They might mention that I "needed to pay attention more" or perhaps that I "needed to pay more attention," which are not the same thing. After they had me in class for a while, they might use different words: "stupid," "troublemaker," "class clown," "space cadet," among others. Then they'd figure out how to get me out of the room. When they figured out that the best way to do this was to send me to a "special" room, my classmates added the inevitable "retard" to the verbal diagnosis.

Many, many years later, a doctor diagnosing me with Attention Deficit-Hyperactivity Disorder would ask me to fill out two copies of a survey. The survey listed all kinds of "behaviors" and asked if I did them.

I was supposed to fill out one survey for what I was like when I was between five and fifteen-years-old and the other for what I was like "as an adult." The doctor also gave me another copy of the survey for my "significant other," which meant the woman I was sleeping with at that point. She only had one version since she didn't know me as a child. One of the behaviors listed was "runs around and climbs inappropriately." I checked "yes" for that on my "child" survey but not on the adult one. My "significant other" checked the "yes" box on the adult list. Both the doctor and I thought that was funny. The woman who was my "significant other" at that point was also a teacher. She would often say, "I just can't imagine having to deal with you in a classroom." She would also say, "I spend most of my time when I'm out with you hoping you won't do or say the first thing that comes into your mind." These comments probably tell you something about me. They certainly should have tipped me off to the fact that our relationship wasn't going to last, but they didn't.

The principal was an enormous man named Mr. Schmuckmin. He was definitely very fat and I think very big as well although it is hard to trust the memories of size from when you are a child. When you are a child lots of things appear big that later prove not to be. It is, as most things are, all a matter of perspective. Mr. Schmuckmin though was definitely fat, cartoon character fat. His body looked like a ball. Plus he was bald and had a big round face, so he looked like a big ball with a smaller ball on top. He drove the first Mercedes-Benz any of us had ever seen. We assumed his size carried great strength. In fact, this was legendary.

Next to the school, just to the east along the Shore Road, was a huge hill. At the top of the hill were three tall apartment buildings. My father had told me that when my brother and oldest sister were young there were abandoned Victorian mansions up there that they would explore on Sunday afternoons. Huge old houses with "widows' walks," the upper porches where wives would watch for their husbands' return from the sea. I was jealous because I had no memory of that. To me those three big buildings had always been there. I had friends who had grown up there. There was a seven-foot basketball hoop up there in the playground – that was the first place me or any of my friends got to dunk.

But between the apartments and the school was a fenced-off part of the hill. It was very fenced off with a twenty-foot high chain-link fence topped with barbed wire. I don't know why this was so off limits because it had all the things the rest of our schoolyard didn't: grass, trees, and rocks to climb on. Once a year they'd let us on it. That is, once a year after you were in fourth grade, three times total. Mr. Schmuckmin would barbecue burgers for lunch and they'd let us eat up on the hill. That was it; being there any other time, except maybe because you were retrieving a baseball hit over that fence from the sixth-grade playground, would get you in lots of trouble.

Anyway, the legend was this. Along the Shore Road there was a gigantic stone wall that held back the hill. Gigantic. Probably forty feet high – maybe more at its highest – although it started at just about two feet right next to the school driveway, so you could easily get to it and walk along the top of the wall, between the fence on one side and the fall on the other. It ran for just about two blocks. If you got caught walking along it you'd get in even more trouble than for getting caught up on the hill; so we only went up there when dared. That's not the legend, of course. The legend was that Mr. Schmuckmin built the wall. By hand. All by himself. That he had carried each of those blocks of granite up there and put them in place. We all believed this absolutely through, probably, third grade. Then, although we had our doubts, we never totally disbelieved it. I doubt Mr. Schmuckmin ever did anything to discourage this belief. After all, this story made him incredibly powerful and thus someone to be feared and this is good when you are in charge of a very large urban elementary school.

Once you got used to being sent to the principal's office you came to realize that, even though you believed the legend, Mr. Schmuckmin was not *that* scary. This happened because he never did hit you – not with his hands that had carried all those stones and not even with the big wooden paddle that he kept leaning against his office wall near the door that led to the AV room. He did yell a lot, but I have found that people who yell at me scare me much less than people who hit me. I think that is true for most people, though clearly not for all.

Part Two: Where

Trinity had been built in the mid-fifties and was overcrowded before it opened. The name actually came from the fact that this building had replaced the city's first public school. "Old Trinity" was a square, red-brick, three-story building from 1823, with a wooden front porch and a belfry complete with bats and a rope for bell-ringing that ran down a pipe to the custodian's basement office. It had blackboards made with inch-thick slabs of slate. Old Trinity was on Trinity Place, a street named for its original inclusion in the church lands that had formed the center of the 17th Century settlement. New Rochelle had been founded by French Protestants, "Huguenots" as they are called, in 1688. When the New World provided good incomes, they became less Calvinist in religious orientation and most of the community joined the Church of England. The original church had become "Trinity." It is still Episcopalian and still occupies the same site, though in an 1850s building now that looks very French and very Catholic. Meanwhile the school, on land the church donated, lived under a variety of names: Trinity School, Trinity Place School, and during the brief infatuation with New York City-style efficiency, Public School Number One. The last remodeling had come in the 1860s after it had served a brief stint as a Civil War hospital. I guess that at some point they had put some bathrooms in the basement, because my sister told me that's where they were. "Old Trinity" sat on beautiful grounds surrounded by giant old maples and sycamores. There was a large "upper playground" that surrounded the building, and then, about sixty or seventy feet down a massive stone staircase was the "lower playground" whose shape and size suggested that it had once served as a playing field back in the 19th Century when the building included all grades through twelfth.

But "New Trinity" had not been built there. Instead, it sat on landfill at the edge of the city's original "mill pond," a spring-fed tidal swamp that Huguenot settlers had dammed to run their first gristmill. The fill was slow to take in the tidal zone and so at first the school had only minimal playgrounds surrounding it, all asphalt paved, even though in the best form of progressive post-war school architecture there were separate playgrounds for different age groups. The school was more than ten-years-old before they managed to push enough dirt, including all the dirt removed for the foundation of the new downtown shopping mall and the debris from all the old downtown buildings torn down for the mall, into the swamp to create a grass play area. It was nice to have even if it flooded a lot and was often swarmed with mosquitoes.

When my oldest sister was in third grade in Old Trinity, they packed all their stuff into shopping bags and walked down Church Street, an enormous hill, from the old school to the new. They walked past the tiny houses that collected along one side, past the iron gates and fence of Isaac E. Young Junior High that had shared a block with the old school, and finally across the Shore Road. My sister said that her third grade teacher wore ankle-length skirts and high-button shoes and looked as if she had been at home in Old Trinity forever, but in the glass-walled classrooms on the tidal flat she seemed hopelessly out-of-place and retired at the end of that year.

By the time I was eleven they had torn the old building down and replaced it with a Little League field. The gigantic maples that had framed and shaded the porch now did the same for the third base bleachers. I played on that field and it was great, but I missed the old building and the bats had to move to drain holes in the multi-story stone wall that faced the adjoining backyard of the apartment house I grew up in. We lived there, all six of us, in a one-bedroom apartment, which made the back yard important even if the bats were now much closer to the chestnut tree – the essential thing to climb.

The destruction of a landmark like that seems inexplicable now, but at the same time in Manhattan they were demolishing Pennsylvania Station, one of the most amazing buildings the country has known and were busy topping Grand Central with the Pan Am Building. It was not a good time for historic preservation. Within a few years, things would change and an abandoned 1905 high school would be renovated beautifully into a grand City Hall, and an 1890s fire station would be rescued as an office building. When I reached adulthood vast public sums would be spent restoring old Main Street facades. This is positive progress, though the old school is gone forever.

When they tore it down my father bought one of the ancient inch-thick slate blackboards at an auction, and though I have no idea how he moved it to our apartment, he did, and for years when I could find myself alone in the kitchen I drew my dreams on it. It survives today in my sister's house, which I suppose is right.

Before the new school was five-years-old they had expanded it. Twelve classrooms were added in a "new wing" that pressed even further into the swamp. The school had been two stories, but the new part had three, starting a half floor lower and going a half floor higher. The "split-level" type stairways made for interesting places those times when you got to wander the halls.

The first grade and kindergarten were in their own wing down past the gym. It was only one story high and all those rooms had their own miniature-sized bathrooms. The two rooms that had been built as kindergartens were amazing. They were huge with windows on two and half sides and water tables and sand tables and even dirt tables for growing things in the glare of the south-facing windows. Early in my kindergarten year, a hurricane rolled in from the Atlantic and sent something flying into one of those windows, cracking it. The principal decided the best course of action, as the storm reached toward us, was to send everyone home from school. We walked through driving wind and rain. We criss-crossed through back yards and holes in fences and under wildly swaying trees some of which stood 70 or 80 feet tall. The next morning we could walk along the trunks of more than a half-dozen of those trees that had crashed to the ground. It is a grand memory.

I want to say this about Attention Deficit-Hyperactivity Disorder. It is not, in my experience, about "attention deficit" at all. This is why I said this is not a good name for what it is. An attention deficit would mean that I was not paying enough attention or that I was not paying attention enough of the time. Neither is true for me. In recent years when I finally began to talk to other people who were said to have Attention Deficit-Hyperactivity Disorder – I found that it usually wasn't true for them either. Someone asked me once what I thought a better name would be. I said that I thought "Attention Discrimination" should be the key words. I said this because I pay attention to just about everything and I'm pretty sure I'm paying attention all the time. If I wasn't, I surely couldn't reach back across all these years and describe all the things I have been describing or will be describing to you. It certainly seems like I was paying very close attention to all kinds of things, seen, heard, and even overheard. So that is not the problem.

The problem is this. Say that you are in a classroom. In that classroom, hundreds of things are happening every minute. People are talking, people are moving, papers are rustling and pages are turning, the air from the ventilator is making the flag move, chairs are squeaking, there may be fish in an aquarium that are swimming while their air pump bubbles or the classroom hamster running on an exercise wheel in its cage, someone will sneeze or cough or drop their pencil and reach down and pick it up or pick lint off their sweater or pass a note to the person next to them – there might be things hanging from the ceiling that are slowly turning, there is dust floating in the sunlight coming through the windows, and of course there are fluorescent lights that are actually, this is true, blinking on and off sixty times every second. Plus, there are probably hundreds of words and dozens of pictures on the walls, each intending to grab your attention, there are patterns in the floor and on the ceiling tiles, there is the grain of the wood on your desktop sometimes marked with scratches and writing that other students have put there, there are books all over the place with words on them and the hardware that holds your notebook together. Then, outside the window and in the hall outside the door are millions of other things – cars and birds and planes and kids at recess and clouds going by, or even more amazing – rain, or a person walking past the classroom door, or just the way that power lines and phone wires hang between each pole. And finally there is everything about you – from the feel of each piece of clothing against your skin to whether you are hot or hungry or thirsty to the tag at the back of your shirt that is scratching your neck to listening to the funny little noise of the blood running through your ears or trying to find a pattern in the weave of the fabric of your jeans and what could be more incredible than the shapes on the bottom of your sneakers and how dirt sticks into them.

All of these things are going on. One of those things might be the teacher talking or one might be the test you are supposed to be taking. But in each of those cases that is still just one thing and there are, obviously, so many things. And the point is that even if I'm supposed to know which of those things I should be paying the most attention to, even if I've been told "five hundred times for God's sake," it still doesn't work. It's still like having a dozen people standing around me all yelling different things at once. Later people told me that because I paid attention to so much stuff it made me a good cop; maybe so, but it does not make you the favorite of any teacher.

Part Three: Why

School was OK in kindergarten. At least that is how I recall it. I may have had trouble with naptime, but this was before kindergarten was all reading and numbers. I could do well with the sand table or the water table. I knew how to use the bathroom and didn't get into too many fights by the swings. I was successful.

Things didn't start to run in the wrong directions until the next year when the teacher brought out something called *The Big Red Reader*, which was probably more than two-feet high and sat on an easel. Then she handed each of us a smaller version, *The Little Red Reader*. This is a famous book. This is the "See Dick run. Run Dick, run." book. The appearance of this book in this classroom changed my life. That is an interesting thought. I think the authors, the publishers, the teachers, everyone involved, would have liked that thought: "We will teach them to read and it will change their little lives." I am certain that was the intent. But they never really considered the other side. They never considered the changes wrought when all those little symbols on all those pages don't add up to anything.

When there is one thing wrong with you in school that is a problem, but when there are two things or more that is something else entirely. And when one of those things that are wrong has to do with reading, well, then you are "special." And "special" is not a good thing.

So, if I couldn't sit still well in first grade or maybe it didn't seem like I was paying attention that was one problem. But then when I couldn't figure out this reading thing, the fact that I couldn't sit still and wasn't paying attention became clues to the teacher. And to the teacher, these clues started to say that I was probably "brain damaged," "retarded," or, at the very least, "slow."

The teacher doesn't put together all those clues at once or necessarily act on them at once. It happens slower than that. Well, not all the time. If you're the kind of kid who drools, for example, or who sits in the corner and bangs your head against the wall, or you fall-over all the time and have seizures this process happens real fast. But for me it was slower. I was not that obvious.

So in this room, on the first grade hall near the corner that led you to the main hall and the gym, which looked out on the first grade playground, which was a tiny raised asphalt terrace maybe eight feet above Church Street Extension, which was where they had pushed Church Street south across the swamp on a causeway so that it was easier for the rich people who lived along the Long Island Sound shore to get to the city and work and shopping, things went wrong, but not, as I said, all at once.

Because at first, lots of kids have a hard time with reading. A lot of adults, especially the kind of adults who do really well in school and become teachers and principals and school board presidents either don't remember or don't understand this, but it is true. Reading, I have since learned, involves lots of complicated symbolic understandings that can be pretty difficult for a young kid's mind. I know that for some it's real easy, but for the rest of us, think about it – you have to memorize twenty-six new symbols that, most often, have two very different ways they might look: A and a, for example, or G and g. Then, you have to memorize which sounds go with each, except that sometimes more than one sound goes with a symbol, which is ridiculous. Then you have to memorize hundreds, then thousands, of ways these symbols interlock with each other to form new combined symbols that are called "words." Then you have to memorize what all those words mean. It is important to know that this is really a code. It is a code because it is not designed to make these understandings easy. If it was, the word "house" might look like a house, which is true in Chinese and in ancient Egyptian, but it is not true for us.

And all of this only gets you to a collection of words. Then you need to learn all sorts of other symbols, like . , : ". These are not words but they mean things too. Then you have to learn that words are put together differently on a page, at least usually, than they are when people speak them. You have to memorize all that and learn all that, and you are only six-years-old, and there are millions of other things demanding your attention – not the least of which are the gulls that wheel outside the classroom window picking up shells from the mill pond and dropping them on the rocks to crack them open.

Maybe if that was the only thing they expected from you at six-years-old, maybe then you might have a chance. After all, the guys who broke the German and Japanese codes in World War II had whole teams of people doing nothing but figuring out the codes and it took them years working in windowless rooms. But they expected more. At the same time, they wanted us to learn numbers, which are other symbols that don't look like anything they mean. And they may have even wanted us to do things with those symbols, like add them up or subtract them, which is just as hard as making words and sentences out of the symbols they call the "alphabet." So they wanted us to learn to decipher two code systems at once, at six-years-old, and then there was even more.

They wanted us to know about clocks and weather names, and about holidays and people like George Washington who were long dead. And they wanted us to sit in that room most of the day, at our desks, and only have two recesses. And we were supposed to remember all kinds of things: like which chair was ours, and which cubby was ours, and the names of teachers and the principal, and what days we had gym. And we didn't spend hardly anytime on the things that had been most important to us until we got to school – running and climbing and playing with bugs and baseball and playing war and riding bicycles and finding our way from here to there.

In my opinion that's an unfair awful lot to put on a six-year-old.

So at first lots of kids had problems, but then, slowly, more and more started figuring it out. As they did they got different books: *The Little Blue Reader*, *The Little Green Reader*, and so on. After a couple of months, the teacher divided the class into "reading groups." She would sit with one group at a time while the rest of us were supposed to be "reading silently," which is a stupid thing to be told if you can't read. I think there were four groups. Each had a different color book showing how far they had gotten. My group still had the red one. We still had the red one at Christmas. We still had the red one at Easter.

This is not just about reading. Something else happens. Up until you are in school kids are rated and ranked by other kids based on a diverse group of things. Where you live, for example, if you live in a big house and everyone else lives in an apartment that means something. What toys you have is another. Having a cool train set or slot cars mattered a lot. I had slot cars. They were my Santa Claus Christmas present when I was five although I really didn't get to play with them at all for days while my dad and brother and cousins raced them all the time. But then I did and that was cool – even if I always had to take the set apart and put them away before dinner because, "There just isn't any room." There might also be what kind of job your father had. Like if your dad worked in the hardware store that could be kind of good. People would know him and know that he worked around cool stuff. My dad played hockey during the winter so that could have been really cool, but he didn't play for the Rangers, he played for the Rovers. The Rovers were a minor league team and so it didn't count nearly as much.

The biggest thing, at least for boys, was how good you were at baseball and hockey and climbing trees. If you were good at that, you were good. As long as you didn't smell really bad all the time or have something weird about you like Frank Geeton who had a "lazy eye."

So I had my ranking, which was pretty good, cause I could climb really well and was OK at baseball and good at hockey; plus, I had slot cars and a dad who played sports. But once the teacher made the reading groups there was a different kind of ranking. Once the teacher made reading groups, I was officially a "dumb kid." This started as a small thing, but school gets more and more important as you get older. And the more important school gets, the more important the school's ranking system gets. Eventually, the very first thing people know about you is that you're a "dumb kid."

Then it got worse.

When it was Lincoln's Birthday and Washington's Birthday, and we were still on the red book, the clues in the teacher's mind started to add up. She decides that she can't do this by herself, which may be fair from her point of view. So she decides to send you to the "specialist," and this, if you are the student, is not fair at all from your point of view. Because if there is one thing no kid wants, it is to get separated out from all the other kids. This is just never good.

It starts innocently enough. The teacher calls your name and asks you to come up to her desk. Then she points to a lady you've never seen before who is standing outside the classroom door. All you can see is her face through the little window. Then she tells you that you have to go with this lady because she's "going to help you," and so you go with her. The other kids start whispering – wondering what's happening to you. At this point, you don't know and they don't know, so it's a mystery. But soon you know and they know. Then it's a label.

That first specialist had those funny eyeglasses that hung from a chain around her neck. They were the kind of glasses where there is a frame on the bottom and sides of the lenses, but not on the top. She smelled, just a little bit, like Mrs. Brown's rose garden. Mrs. Brown lived in a tiny house on Trinity Place, around the corner from us, and was a friend of my mother. Except for a few narrow walks, every bit of her property from the house out to the fences was covered with flowers. In the front was almost nothing but roses. And the specialist smelled just a little bit like that. On that first day and on other days after, I would follow her down the hall. We would go to a little room off the nurse's office that was otherwise mostly used for hearing tests. You know where you wear the big headphones and raise your hand as you hear each sound. But they only had hearing tests once a year so the rest of the time the room was mostly available. Like most schools built in the 1950s or before Trinity wasn't built with any rooms for specialists. This wasn't part of education back then I guess. I don't know what they did with kids like me before there were specialists – and I don't know whether whatever they did would have been better or worse.

In that little room there was just a desk and two chairs. There were no windows, but air blew through a grating up by the ceiling. The walls were that strange color green you see only in hospitals or maybe college dorms. There was a poster showing what was inside an ear. The fluorescent lights, in such a small space, buzzed loudly. The specialist sat on one side of the desk and I sat on the other. There were many books and papers on the desk, and in one corner a stack of file folders, and some yellow pads.

At first, the specialist had me try to read to her, but that didn't go well. Then she tried to have me read something by using a piece of cardboard that had a rectangle cut out that allowed me to see just one word at a time. I think she was trying to help me with distractions, but that really didn't work any better. Then she showed me a chart of the alphabet with all capital letters and asked me to read it, and I could because I knew the alphabet. Then she showed me the same kind of chart only with small letters and I must have made some mistakes because she said "umm," "oh," and "go on" a lot, and wrote many things on a yellow pad. This was my first lesson in how people look at you when you fail tests that you're not supposed to fail. When they are "professionals" as the specialist was they try to make this not obvious, but they cannot do it. Most are compelled, I guess, to take notes and this is a give-away. All though, get a certain look in their eyes and you know you've failed. The specialist looked like that and said that we'd get together again soon, which I didn't really understand, and she walked me back to my class.

Eventually, I had to meet with the specialist a couple of times a week. And I hated this. There was nothing that I was supposed to do when I was with her that wasn't either incredibly hard or totally impossible. Plus, the lights and the buzz and room made my head hurt, and eventually, the specialist's smell of roses made me feel sick after I'd been in the room for just a few minutes. Then I'd feel sick walking down the hall with her. Then I'd feel sick if I even knew it was getting close to the time when she would come for me.

On the other hand, the specialist thought I was making progress. She thought this because I had figured out my first trick – I realized that all either the specialist or my teacher wanted was for me to be able to read *The Little Red Reader*. I couldn't do that, but I found out that I didn't have to. I had heard this book so many times that I realized I had it memorized. But there was something else. I couldn't just repeat the story to the specialist or the teacher, because I knew that only parts of it were on each page and that you could only read what was on the page in front of you. So I carefully started matching up my memory of the words with the pictures on each page. Then I could look at the pictures, remember the words, say them, and have everyone assume I was reading. This was decoding too, but I had decoded different things. And this worked; by the end of the year the specialist and the teacher were sure they had made a difference. If I was "slow," I was at least "teachable." They said I could go on to second grade and let me out for the summer.

It was not a good summer. I don't mean it was all bad, just that it was not all good. One good thing was going to school for two years had made the world bigger. I'd proved that I could cross all kinds of streets. I'd met kids and made friends from far beyond the apartments I lived in, or the street I lived on, or even the giant block that the apartments and Old Trinity and the junior high were on. Another good thing was that New Rochelle, at least my end, was a pretty cool summer place. There were beaches and rocks along the shore and swamps and ponds, all of which make great summer days when you are seven. On the longest days my friends and I could ride our bikes as far as the beach at Hudson Park or the ferry to Fort Slocum. We could swim in the Sound or we could play baseball for endless hours on the lower field of Old Trinity. At some point, we'd make a serious effort to collect Coke bottles we could return to Seif's on Church Street so we could buy our own Cokes and candy. Or if we were at Hudson Park, we'd return them to Dudley's, which was down by the boatyard. Seif's was a little grocery attached to the front of an old house at the corner of Union Street. The pull bar on the screen door had a picture of the lady from the Old Dutch Cleanser can and on the left side of the store was a long counter that had nothing but candy in it, though there were newspaper racks and a shelf full of Wonder Bread in front of it. In the corner to the right when you first came in was the Coke cooler – one of those big red ones that you had to reach down into from the top, which is a stretch when you are seven. But on a hot day reaching in there for a Coke was the best thing. At the candy counter, I'd usually get dots, those little colored candies stuck on the strip of paper. They were both cheap and took a long time to eat, which was good.

So with all that, I should be able to say it was a good summer but it wasn't. For my father that past winter had been his last playing hockey. He didn't want to quit, but the Rangers had decided he'd never make it to the National Hockey League so there was no room for him anymore on their farm team. The Rangers had been bad for years and now they were trying to get younger and better and my father didn't fit into those plans. I guess he could have hooked on with a lower-level team somewhere else, but I also guess this seemed ridiculous: "At his age and with a family to support." So he just decided to give it up and work all year long at the beer distributor where he usually worked between seasons. At first, this seemed OK and there wasn't really anything different. But then as summer went along I think my father realized that he wasn't going back to training camp, and he wasn't going back to the team, and he wasn't going to get to play hockey and travel all around anymore, and that he was now stuck delivering beer as a full-time job. I mean, I think that now, at the time I really didn't think about this at all. I did notice that he started coming home much later, that he was drunk a lot more, that he and my mother yelled at each other a lot. And my mom started working more – I guess because money was going to be "even tighter." She worked at Bloomingdale's, which was a big department store up on Main Street with six floors and escalators. Now she would work Saturdays and Thursday nights, which she had never done before. And now, pretty much the only time my mom and dad would see one another, they would fight.

In a one bedroom apartment with six people there is no place to get away when two people are fighting so I would do the only things I could, either hide under my bed or just go outside. When I went outside, I would usually cut through the hole in the back fence into the lower field of Old Trinity – then I would climb up the old stone staircase which you had to be really careful of in the dark because it was pretty much a mess with lots of stones out of place and big plants growing up between other stones. And I would sit on the porch of the old school under the huge maples. I would look up at the stars – you could see them because there were no lights around, except the few streetlights on Trinity Place, and the big trees above those kept that light from going up into the sky. This is one reason why I was sad when they tore the old school down.

Then one night I came home. Neither my mother or father or brother Mike were there, just my sisters, which was strange because it was very late and things had usually "settled down by then." My sister Karen was cleaning up in the kitchen wiping something off the front of the refrigerator, which turned out to be my mother's blood from where my father had hit her and she had fallen back and bashed her head. So my parents had gone to the hospital. I wasn't sure where Mike had gone. Mom stayed at the hospital for three days. Mike didn't come home for more than a week. It took me four years to learn that he had hit my father that night after my father hit my mother.

After a while everyone was back home, but things were different, and the closer the hockey season came the sadder my dad got, and the sadder he got the more he stayed "at the bar," though I didn't know where that was, and the more he stayed at the bar the more afraid of him I got when he came home, which I had never been before.

So second grade started like that. And with it came a whole new part of the school. The second grade classrooms stretched along the first floor of the opposite side of the "U." One side of the hall, the inside of the shape, was all classrooms with doors from each opening out into the big central playground. There were some classrooms on the other side of the hall, but most of that side was filled by the cafeteria, which was where we went for recess when it rained. Most of us didn't eat lunch in the cafeteria; we went home. We went home for lunch even if no parent was home. That seems strange to kids now, they are used to short lunches and long bus rides, but New Rochelle was just about ten and a half square miles and had twelve elementary schools, each representing a distinct neighborhood, and none involving busses. So it was a pretty small cafeteria with just a tiny kitchen and I don't remember that they ever made any food there.

Across the hall from the door to the kitchen there was a set of double doors. Big wooden double doors with little aluminum letters on one that said "B O O K R O O M." But it was not really a room. It was more like a big closet. On my first day of school, I noticed this because it was right next to Mrs. Wilson's room, which was where I would be for second grade. On the second day, there were sixth grade boys in that room and they were taking big piles and boxes of books out. But by that day – I had other things to worry about.

Mrs. Wilson was not a nice person. She didn't even pretend to be a nice person. At some point you wonder why someone who seems to hate kids so much would become a teacher and Mrs. Wilson seemed to hate kids. By the second day, she had already hit me twice with a yardstick, both times for getting up from my seat. Mrs. Wilson's room was especially hard to sit still in because its windows faced the playground. Different grades had different recesses and four grades used that playground so almost all of the time there were kids outside that window playing. But even if there weren't any kids out there, there were the windows of all the other classrooms that faced the playground. And more. If you turned around, away from the blackboard, the view included the whole sweep of the swamp and the mill pond and the cars on the causeway. It was a very big scene. I had to turn around. I had to look. None of that made it so bad. What made it so bad was that Mrs. Wilson would hold onto her yardstick all day, and if she was not smacking it into kids, she was smacking it on desks, or on the blackboard, on anything. The sound was horrible. I became sure that every smack was directed at me and I just couldn't sit there.

By the end of the third week, I would come into the class and hide in the back corner by the windows. I would ball myself up there on the floor. At first, this brought on more hitting: on my thighs, on my butt, on my hands. Then, sometimes, Mrs. Wilson would drag me out of the corner and put me in the closet. I decided that was OK. Once the closet door was shut I could not see her and she could not hit me. Things might have just gone along like that, but then the air raid drills began.

Now I can see those weeks of October 1962 in a different light, in a historical view. Now I can laugh at the absurdity of our attempts at survival in a nuclear war. We were in a glass building with no basement fifteen miles from Times Square. Actually, it was worse than that, though nobody knew it then not even the adults. Fort Slocum had been turned into a missile base. This was a secret, and it never got publicly revealed until years later when Fort Slocum was abandoned and given to the city, and someone read the environmental report. So if Cuba had blown up and the world had blown up with it – we would have been among the first to go. But apparently, they still wanted to try. The adults were absolutely panicked in their commitment to try. And, like adults do, they spread their panic to us.

So the sirens would go off. A constant wail unlike any other bell or alarm. One that didn't stop and let you catch your breath or stop and think. Then we'd all have to, "Very quickly now children, but don't run," get into the hallway and sit rolled up into little balls facing the wall, "Away from any glass now!" and be absolutely silent.

But what are you supposed to do if where the teacher pushed you was right under a cabinet in the wall with a fire extinguisher in it and there was a glass door in front of the fire extinguisher? And you had to try and get up to say, "There's glass here," because you know from all those World War II movies on TV that the glass will shatter and fall on you and cut you, and the teacher who you don't know who is yelling in the hall, has even said, "Away from any glass?" And what are you supposed to do when Billy Shantz that little creep starts poking you and saying, "Why don't you just stay in your corner and get blown up?" and he just keeps poking you and saying that? And what are you supposed to do when Mrs. Wilson forgets that she has put you in the closet and the siren is going off and you don't know whether to come out of the closet or not and so you don't, but then the siren is still going and so you do, and then you walk out into the hall when everybody else is already balled up in position, and you are, "Opening doors and walking around"?

Apparently, you could do many things, but one of them was not messing up air raid drills. So one day in early November I was brought next door – to the Book Room.

The Book Room had changed. It was no longer a closet. It was no longer for storage. Now it was a kind of an office and, like the little office next to the nurse's office, it had no window. Like that little office it was lit by buzzing fluorescent lights, but it was much bigger than that room. There were still big metal shelves along the two side walls, but marks on the floor showed where other shelves had been taken out of the middle of the space. Across the middle of the room, dividing it front and back, was a wall – though it didn't go all the way up to ceiling. It also didn't go quite all the way across. So there was kind of a doorway. The wall had pictures on it, one of a lake, one of a forest. In front of the wall was a desk, a desk chair and two soft chairs, like you might have in a living room. I could see part of a couch behind the wall.

A lady, who I assumed was another "specialist," had taken me from my classroom to the Book Room. She had come into the classroom and walked back to the corner where I was and had bent her knees until she was just a little above me and had asked if I would come and talk to her. Her voice was soft: It wasn't angry – but it still took a little while before I would answer her. She was much younger than last year's specialist and she didn't have glasses and I don't remember her smelling strange. And I think I nodded instead of saying anything. I walked out of the classroom with her as all the other kids were whispering and Mrs. Wilson was smacking her yardstick down on her desk to get them to be quiet. In those weeks in Mrs. Wilson's class I had given up caring about what the other kids were whispering about me. I knew they were whispering and talking, but it didn't matter. I had stopped doing anything at recess –

either Mrs. Wilson wouldn't let me go out, or if she did, I would just stand by the fence, stare at the swamp, and not talk to anyone. I had stopped going home for lunch too. Instead, I would just go across Church Street from the school and would hide behind the apartment building there and look at the mill pond. I even found a place there with a roof so I could hide there on rainy days. But I hadn't stopped caring about Mrs. Wilson's yardstick, and even as I walked out of the room with the new specialist, I flinched each time she hit it against the desk.

I assumed that I was going to the Book Room to work on reading and this made me scared. I tried to remember *The Little Red Reader* but I couldn't. For weeks, I hadn't paid attention to any book in class; I didn't know anything about second grade books. All the tricks I had worked out to look like I was "making progress" last year were going to be useless.

But the lady didn't want to talk about reading. At least not that first day. She took me past the wall and let me sit on the couch. In the back there were pictures of boats and a picture of a beach that looked a little like one of the beaches at Hudson Park. She asked me if I wanted something to drink, and I nodded, and she gave me a small carton of orange drink. Then she sat in a living room kind of chair that faced the couch. There was another desk, another desk chair in the corner, and a coffee table between us that had books and magazines on it. Two of the magazines were *Highlights* and one was a *Life* from last spring that I had looked at in the barbershop on North Avenue. It had pictures of the Mets in it. The *Highlights* reminded me of doctors' offices and I wondered if this lady was a doctor, but that didn't make sense. And we sat there and didn't say anything for what seemed like a long time.

Then the lady said, "I hear you've been having a hard time." And I said, "I can't read," mostly because I thought that was what this was about. But she said, "I don't know if that's true, but I don't think that's what's the matter."

And that was my first time in the Book Room.

I would spend a lot of time there. Usually I would be in the Book Room for some period of time every day. It is hard though to remember for how long each day. There were no big clocks in the Book Room only small ones, like travel alarm clocks that sat discreetly on the desks, always aimed so that, as a student, you could not read them. Without windows and with the stale, hot air that came from, "Keeping the door closed for privacy," time was pretty much a mystery. I didn't have a watch at seven. I didn't know any seven-year-old who had a watch. Later, when other kids got watches I did not. I still only wear them occasionally. I do not like things wrapped around my wrist like that and I have found, that even if I have a watch on I forget to look at it – so I am as equally likely to be early or late, and I am early or late to almost everything with a watch or without.

At first I could only judge my time in the Book Room by how much less time I had to spend in Mrs. Wilson's room. And this was hard as well since I did nothing in Mrs. Wilson's room, but sit in the corner. After I started going to the Book Room Mrs. Wilson put me in the closet a lot less. Later, I realized that this was because she didn't want the lady from the Book Room to come to get me and find me in the closet. But, obviously, I did not know that then. There was no effect, however, on the number of times in a day that Mrs. Wilson would hit me with the yardstick, which remained at just about three on typical days, rising to five or six on bad ones.

Still, I knew I was in Mrs. Wilson's room less. I heard the yardstick less. And this was good. At some point, it was later in the year after Christmas vacation, the lady from the Book Room told me that if I got "too scared" in Mrs. Wilson's classroom, I should just tell Mrs. Wilson that I had to go next door and I should come to the Book Room. But I never did. I was also told that "one goal" I should have was to try and sit in my chair more in class and "pay attention" to Mrs. Wilson, even if at first I could only do that for "one half hour" at a time. I was supposed to be, "Working toward that goal," and so I tried. At least once a week, after a couple of weeks of going to the Book Room, I would try – at the beginning of the day or just after lunch – to sit in my chair. Sometimes, I could make it for one half hour, though it was a struggle to pay attention to anything Mrs. Wilson was doing, except for the fact that she was smacking her yardstick on someone or something every two minutes.

One thing I learned that year was that it was important to try to do the things that adults gave you as "goals." If you tried, it meant that you were being "compliant." And if you are being "compliant" the adults involved or the people in authority when you are older, will keep talking to you and "working with you" and being nice to you. If you are not "compliant," different things happen.

I added knowing about compliance to what I had learned in first grade, which was that I had to be "making progress." I had also learned that a good memory could get you through a lot. These have proved to be essential life skills.

So, as the year went on, I tried to sit at my desk as much as I could, which wasn't very much time, but I'm pretty sure the time kept getting longer. And while I was sitting at my desk, I would try to listen and remember something, though I never gave an answer to Mrs. Wilson. I would tell the lady in the Book Room some of those things I remembered, which would let her report that I was learning – that I could learn. I was making lots of progress.

Part Four: Who

There were, at this point in time, only three rooms on the second floor of the school that I knew about. One was the library, which I had liked in first grade, because of all the books with pictures, but which Mrs. Wilson would not let me go to because I had not read enough books in her class. In fact, I hadn't read any. Mrs. Wilson kept track of how many books you had read on a bulletin board on one of the coat closet doors. The board had a blue background and was supposed to look like water. On the bottom was a wavy border of brown and yellow that was supposed to be mud. On the top were little white circles that were supposed to be bubbles. On the water was one fish-shaped piece of gray paper for every student in the class. Your fish had your name written on it in Magic Marker. On one side were numbers starting from "1," at the bottom, and counting up. At first, all the fish were on the bottom, but as the year progressed most of the fish moved up. If you hadn't moved up fast enough you were not allowed to go to the library. My fish remained in the mud, on the bottom, the whole year. So when the class went to the library each week I was sent to go sit in the main office on a little bench alongside the frosted glass.

Another room was the "Home Ec" room, which was like five or six big kitchens all in one place. I had only been in that room once, in first grade, when sixth grade girls made us pumpkin-shaped and colored cookies at Halloween. That room was next to the Library, up above the cafeteria.

The last room that I knew on the second floor was above the music room. It was the art room. It was huge – with windows along two sides looking out over both the hill and the Shore Road. It was the only room in the school with windows facing the Shore Road. We had gone to the art room, mostly to finger paint, maybe once or twice each month in first grade. But Mrs. Wilson would usually not let me go now because I wasn't, "doing my class work." This meant another time that I was expected to sit on the bench in the office while the class did something else. Usually the only other kid there was another second grader who sat rocking back and forth on a chair with his head in his lap and with his arms wrapped around his ears. He had been in my first grade class. I knew his name and I was sure that he knew mine. But he never said anything to me or to anyone else.

After spending many days on the bench by the frosted glass, one of the two secretaries in the office seemed to start to like me and sent me to run errands. "Could you please bring this note to Mrs. Smith's room?" At first, she would draw me a little map showing me how to get there. Then she wouldn't need to do that anymore and she would tell me that I "knew my way around as well as any student in school."

Then around the middle of winter I started to get to go to art. A few weeks later, waiting for the bell before school, Kathy Beerman – who had been in my class all three years – told me that she had overheard people yelling about me in the principal's office one day during lunch when she had gotten sick and was waiting for her mother to come and pick her up. She thought that there were three people yelling, Mr. Schmuckmin, Mrs. Wilson, and the lady from the Book Room. She heard it, "Made clear," that I was, "…supposed to get to go to art and music and recess pretty much no matter what." Kathy had told me this over by the fence. She had said that she wanted me to know but was telling no one else.

And I liked art. I drew pictures of baseball and hockey players and especially cars. I really liked to draw cars. Sometimes I drew pictures of astronauts in space; and, like at least half the boys in the 1960s, I wanted to be an astronaut. And in the spring, we got to do stuff with clay and I made both an Indy racecar and a Mercury capsule and they went into the kiln. Then we got to paint them with glaze and they went back into the kiln. They came out with the colors all run together – but I still liked them a lot.

Some of the pictures I drew in art ended up in the Book Room, which I thought was strange. The lady would sometimes ask me about the pictures. When she did, she would write on a yellow pad while I answered. She began by asking me questions about why I had drawn this or that, but then she wanted to talk about my car pictures. My car pictures were as exact as I could make them. Lots of kids drew made-up cars, but I always drew real cars and tried to get everything I remembered about the car into the picture. This was a lot because I knew all about cars and I told the lady that. I told her that for as long as I could remember I could pretty much walk down the street and name every car there was, and a lot of times, I would know what year it was too. She asked how I knew all that and I said that I listened to my father. That my father knew all about cars. That every year my father and I went down into New York with my brother Mike and went to the Auto Show, and that whenever I heard anyone say something about a car I remembered it. But I don't think she really believed me because she took me for a walk one day through the teachers' parking lot and she asked me to name all the cars. She seemed really surprised that I could, with no mistakes, including the "Auto-Union," which was a German car that almost nobody knew anything about.

A few days later she did this: She showed me a piece of paper. On it were a bunch of words she had typed and she wanted me to read the words, but I couldn't. I could tell she either was confused, or was getting angry, and I didn't understand. Then she took me back outside again, and she held the paper up against the back of a 1961 Chevrolet Bel-Air four-door hardtop, and she asked if I could find a word on the paper that was the same as the word on the back of the car, but I couldn't, and I thought she was going to get really angry. And she pointed to one word on the paper and asked if that wasn't the same, but it wasn't and I couldn't tell her that it was.

Here is what I think she had typed on the paper. I think she had put words like Ford, Chevrolet, Pontiac, Studebaker, Chrysler, Dodge, Buick, Mercury and maybe more on the paper. I think she was pointing to Chevrolet. But the word on the back of the car looked like this: CHEVROLET, and that cannot be the same. I think she tried with

"Mercury" too, but that car had Mercury on it, which is also not the same. We stood there in the parking lot, by the backs of the cars, and she didn't say anything for a long time and I didn't know what to do. It is bad when you are not yet eight and you obviously need help and you are disappointing just about the only person who is trying to help you. And I must have looked very scared because she finally looked at me and said, "hmmm," and then she put her hand on my shoulder which I didn't really like, but didn't complain about because I knew she was trying to be nice, and she said, "You are an unusual little man," and we went back inside.

It was a week before she brought the subject back up. She took out a different piece of paper. On it were pieces of magazine pages. On the pieces were words from pictures of the back or front or sides of cars, but cut out — so you couldn't see any other part of the cars. She asked me to read the words. And though I didn't think it was reading I told her, "Studebaker, Chevrolet, Cadillac, Mercury, Ford, Chrysler, Rambler," and she said "excellent" and wrote down many things on a yellow pad.

That spring we didn't go to the Auto Show. My father didn't say anything. My sister said there wasn't enough money for silly things like that. My brother Mike told me we'd make our own Auto Show instead. So one Saturday we rode our bikes to every car dealer in New Rochelle. We looked at hundreds of cars, including the Chevrolet Corvair Monza Spyder convertible turbo, which was my favorite, and most of the men at the dealers were really nice and let me take home copies of the fancy magazines with the pictures of all the cars in them. Except at the Pontiac dealer way across town over by Weyman Avenue. We got there late and tired and they chased us away, and said they didn't need kids wasting their time.

And that same spring Mr. Kelleher, who was the boys' gym teacher at Trinity, got me on the second grade, after-school, baseball team. That was as organized as baseball got back then — if you were less than ten-years-old. We played games against the other elementary schools using one of the fields at the junior high since we had no place at our school. I almost always played third base and I hit one home run. This helped be-cause when I was playing baseball I wasn't just the retard in the corner. At the end of the season I had to give back the T-shirt that said "Trinity," but I got to keep the yellow hat with the blue "T," which I ended up wearing almost as much as the Mets hat I had from the year before.

And the school year sort of drifted away. On my final report card, it said many things that were written in cursive, which I certainly couldn't read, but Kathy Beerman did look at it on the way home and told me it said that I would be in third grade the next year, so I had gotten past that.

Part Five: How

Over the next two years, I went to the Book Room just about every day that I went to school. I would go in the morning and work on reading or arithmetic. I would go in the afternoon and work on "making progress," or take one of the endless tests that were part of life in the Book Room. There were tests with blocks, and tests with puzzles, and tests with questions that most often had to be read to me. There were academic tests, and intelligence tests, and I'm pretty sure personality tests, though those just seemed bizarre to me at that age. And they'd try things with me in the Book Room. They tried glasses with different colored lenses, blue and green, even though I don't wear glasses. This made stuff look funny but did nothing. They tried big sheets of paper with "250 words" that I was supposed to "look and say." I think the idea was to memorize the shapes of words and this may have helped some. They tried changing the way I held a pencil to make my writing better, but that was too hard. They even tried to get me to write with my left hand because they said I had a dominant right eye and so should be left-handed, and the fact that I wasn't meant that I was "laterally confused." Writing with my left hand made me very confused. They tried a machine that projected words up on a screen and showed me just one word at a time, kind of like the rose-smelling lady had that first day in the room off the nurse's office. This was supposed to help my eyes learn to "track properly" and was supposed to "speed up my reading." It did neither. And they kept trying. It sounds cruel now, it sounds ridiculous, but that was as much as people knew back then and they were trying. I shouldn't complain.

My days were like this: I would go to my classroom, on the ground floor of the new wing for third grade, and on the top floor of the new wing for fourth grade, and then I would go to the Book Room, and then I'd come back. There would be lunch and then I'd do the same thing again. Sometimes they would change my schedule around specials: music, art, gym, because there seemed to be "general agreement" that it was "important" for me to go to those. I even started to play the trumpet in the school band, which caused more confusion and many more notes on yellow pads, when it was discovered that I was successfully reading music.

In the Book Room we spent a great deal of time talking about my "home life." There was a great deal of concern about that. Things had surely gone downhill. There was a lot of fighting and I had taken to sleeping under my bed more or less permanently. Then sometime in November of third grade, my father reached to push my mother. I stepped between them and what seemed very much like a punch hit me. This caused my father to run out of the house and my mother to scream and me to go under the bed and not come out, until I could sneak out very early in the morning and go to school, not having eaten or slept, with a large black and blue welt on my face. And because this had never happened before I didn't have a story. It turned out that I never developed good stories for this – although I knew plenty of kids who took it much worse at home and had great stories. It's not that I'm not good at lying; I can lie with the best of them in most situations, but it never worked for me here.

So when first my teacher and then the lady from the Book Room asked me what happened, I more or less told them. And there were, I think, many phone calls and conversations. But this being 1963, not much in the way of anything actually happened because people didn't interfere in families back then. I told them the next couple of times things like that happened too. And there were more phone calls and more conversations, and the lady from the Book Room talked to me a lot about "safe places" and "being safe," and there were lots of questions, but going home kept getting worse.

My time in the classroom was better. My teachers not only didn't hit, they rarely yelled. Sometimes they were even patient. My third grade teacher didn't even try books with me at first but showed me the backs of baseball cards, where we both discovered that I could easily tell her that "NY(N)" meant (New York, National League), which either meant the Giants through 1957 or the Mets from 1962 on. And I also knew what "RBI" stood for (Runs Batted In), and about many other symbols, which she told me *was* reading. She actually told me that I already knew lots of words and that there was no doubt that I'd keep learning more. In classrooms like that it was easier to stay in my seat longer. With teachers that never put me in the closet it was easier to hear them talking amidst all the other things.

When I could hear the teachers talking, I found that sometimes what they were saying made sense. I liked history stories, for example, and once in a while, I would ask questions or even know answers. I liked hearing about other states and other countries. And though I could never quite get it written down right, I started to understand some arithmetic. In fourth grade, we did a class project on architecture and I discovered that I could figure out blueprints when lots of kids couldn't. So I was sure I was making progress. And I was sure I was being compliant. And my memory was getting better and better, and thus, getting more useful. But one thing a kid never knows is what's working against him. There's no way you could know.

The papers had piled up. They had been piling up for four years. There is no real way to stop that from happening: reports, notes, IQ tests, achievement tests, reading tests, math tests, personality profile tests, spatial relationship tests, functional reasoning tests, tests of phonological understanding, of word recognition, of digit span, and more reports, and hundreds more notes, and comments, and progress reports. The papers had piled up. The papers started to take control.

Years later, I met a priest in The Bronx. A Jesuit from Fordham University down near the Botanical Gardens. He would help me with some simple things, including learning to accept things that were, so I could move on. He would become both mentor and tutor, and worked with me endlessly, when I needed to study in the Police Academy. One of the things he told me was that a society should be judged on that which it did for the least among them. I accept that as truth and yet, obviously, I know that it is not really so in the world of humans. Here resources are finite, investments are made in the people most likely to "pay off," and choices have to be made.

In schools, filled for the most part with well-intentioned souls, these choices are left to the piles of papers. It is less painful that way. "There is really no choice in the matter."

For four years enormous resources had been expended on me: A thousand hours? Fifteen hundred hours? Two thousand hours? Dedicated, one-on-one, expensive "specialist" hours. The questions had to come: "To what end?" and "How much more?"

So, in the spring of the year I was in fourth grade, as bulldozers pushed the rubble from the mall site into the swamp and I began to play Little League baseball, and my father started a new job that had had him "on the road" and gone from home for weeks at a time, the lady in the Book Room started me on one more round of tests. The Book Room had changed again over the three years. There were rugs on the floor. The big metal bookcases had disappeared. There was a real door separating the front and back rooms. Even the letters "B O O K R O O M" had been peeled off and replaced by a black plastic sign with white letters that said "SPECIAL SERVICES." And I would go in every day and take one test or another.

No adult told me why I was taking these tests, but there were now other ways to find these things out. A community had developed among the kids of the Book Room. It was, of course, not a community anyone wished to be associated with; and even if it had been possible to avoid it, it would have been unwise. There was information within this community. There were kids who were older who might not only know about this test or that, but might know what it all meant as well. At seven or at eight those meanings would have been both useless and beyond comprehension, but as I turned ten I had begun to need to know.

You couldn't ask just anyone. There was a wide range of capabilities within the community of the Book Room. There were many students who I, trying to feel superior whenever I could, would refer to as "morons." Though I think I tried not to do this to their face. I had to rely on kids I thought were like me, kids who were functioning, kids who were holding on. And they had to be older, in fifth or sixth grade, because only then would they know what had gone on and what was coming.

"Things are changin' little boy, you better watch you ass and do better than they expect." Joey Mostone said this to me as we fielded grounders before a Little League game. Joey was in fifth grade and he had heard things I had not. He was the second baseman and smaller than me, even though he was more than a year older. "What's changing?" I asked. "There gonna be new rooms next year," he mumbled quietly so it was just between us, "and yous gotta stay out'a the drool room."

I stopped, just stopped. I don't think I looked at Joey or anything really — just kind of froze and stared. The ball the fat first base coach had hit to me went through my legs and the scream followed, "Pay attention you little retard!" And I turned and chased the ball.

Joey and I were never friends. In later years there'd be more than a few times that we'd end up at the same parties, but with different friends. We just knew each other the way kids do. And we had similar schedules in the Book Room. We would pass each other coming in and out; sometimes, he would be in one half and I would be in the other. This put us in the community on the same side of things. It didn't seem like he would be messing with me.

In the third inning I sat next to him on the bench. "What is the fuckin' drool room?" I used "fuck," which was not yet really in my vocabulary, to sound older and crazier and more acceptable. He held up two fingers. "Two rooms," he told me. Then, dropping his voice, making it barely audible, "One for the droolers – they'll get locked in all day," he spat on the ground, "The other they'll let ya go to regular classes some time." He stared at me. "Be upstairs wit the fifth and sixth grades, not that bad." Then he picked up a bat and walked out to the on-deck circle.

He didn't say anything else about it the rest of the year, except this — each time we passed, as I was leaving the Book Room and he was coming in, he would let a little whistle escape from between his teeth and say, "Little boy, you best be doin' better." For the rest of his life he would call me "little boy" even though I would always be taller. He even called me "little boy" on that last night, when I was a junior in high school and he was a senior. Me and my friends ran into Joey and his friends on North Avenue by the New Haven Railroad tracks. The street crossed over the tracks on a bridge so old that there were wooden boards under the asphalt. I don't know what brought us all there at two in the morning but it surely involved drinking. "Wo! Little boy!" Joey yelled from where he stood on top of the plate girder that supported the bridge, "How ya doin?" After I answered he slurred, "Ya know, little boy and me go all the way back to the Book Room." And I said, "Long time mo'fucker." And he said something like, "Yeah."

There was that night among Joey's friends a dare. Joey had been dared that he could not cross over the tracks, all five tracks – the four of the New York-to-Boston mainline plus the station siding – by means of one of the ancient steel structures that held up the electric power lines for the trains. The trains here being electric: whether commuter cars, or Amtrak Metroliners, or freights hauled by big locomotives. But unlike the subways in the city which got their power from an electrified third rail off to the side of the track, and which were called – I knew this even then – "low-voltage," these trains were powered by overhead "high-voltage" wires. These terms are apparently relative; touching the subway's low-voltage third rail will kill you instantly.

What Joey was supposed to cross was a kind of bridge, made of criss-crossed pieces of steel riveted together, kind of a latticework square tube that spanned the tracks and held the support wires that, in turn, held the power lines. Some of these also had the railroad signals on them. I do not know if this one was one like that or not.

There really isn't much more to say. I didn't stay. Perhaps I was more high than drunk and so more paranoid. Whatever. One of my friends said something about this being "stupid," We waved and moved off. Not that far. When we heard the sirens, we knew immediately.

This was not the first death from the Book Room. Just the year before Tommy Ippolito had taken out six phone poles over by the college with his brother Ralph's Camaro. It is sad, but very true, that we were all more surprised that Ralph's car had gotten going that fast on that short a street than we were that Tommy was dead.

But, of course, Tommy's wasn't the first death either.

The rumors spread and panic came to the Book Room. The adults remained silent and the tests went on. There were too many questions and very, very, few answers. Those of us involved got angry. Kids from the Book Room started getting into lots of fights both with each other and with the other kids who knew the rumors too, and who would taunt us by saying, "They's gonna put you away retard," and, "You're gonna fail those tests moron and they're gonna lock you up in the drool room," and "I hear they're making a special school just for you retards so you don't contaminate the rest of us."

Kathy Beerman tried to bring news: "It's gonna be all right." She had come up behind me in the corner of our fourth grade classroom, back by the sink. Over the years, now five, that we had been in class together she had become the only "regular" kid I could trust, and she was also nice. Maybe, I had to think in that moment, she was only trying to be nice. "The bad room is gonna be mostly for kids who aren't even here now, kids that can't even eat by themselves, you know, kids who can't walk and stuff. You won't go there. It'll be OK." I walked over to the pencil sharpener and she followed, our words now hidden by the grinding. "How come nobody'll say anything then? How come all these tests again?" "Cause nobody talks to kids," she said. "They think we're all idiots." I stopped sharpening, then somehow dropped the pencil. The point broke off as it hit the floor. "I know they think I'm an idiot," I said. I left the pencil where it had fallen and walked back to my desk. There was nothing I was going to write anyway.

This is what it had come down to. We were no longer trying to be like the regular kids. We were left trying not to be as bad as it got. Faced with this, I now think it's amazing that so many of us kept trying.

I know I did. I really tried and I cheated whenever I could. The main Book Room lady and the other lady were always going to meetings now. The tests were being given by student teachers and what did they know. Sometimes I had seen a test, or been asked the questions, two or three times already – this was especially true of the IQ tests. That had to help. As an adult, I have seen plenty of studies that say it does. One Saturday morning I ran into Johnny Doogan, who was in sixth grade, in Grant's on Main Street. I was looking at model cars in the basement toy department and he and Tommy Ippolito were stealing model glue. Johnny said that it didn't really matter about how you did on the written arithmetic or the questions of "general knowledge," which meant knowing school stuff, or the vocabulary questions or even the thing called "coding," where you had to replace a sign with a shape or a number. We were, he said, supposed to do badly on those. But you had to do better on stuff that showed you weren't a complete idiot, like when they ask: "What would you do if you had a nosebleed?" or, "Why do we have an army?" or when they'd ask, "In what way are a tomato and an apple alike?" And it was good if you did well on the picture stuff – when you'd have to arrange the pieces of a comic book story in order, or they'd show you a picture of a car with only three wheels and ask you what is missing. And also the block stuff where they'd ask you to make a certain thing out of the blocks. Doing well on all of this, Johnny said, would make them decide that you were "worth their time," cause if you couldn't do that stuff you obviously weren't. If Johnny was right this gave me a shot, since I knew I was pretty good at those things.

I tried in class too. I even kept a book with me a lot. It wasn't much really, a kids' condensed version of *Fear Strikes Out,* about a baseball player whose family is all screwed up and who goes crazy, but then sort-of gets better. I was reading it, at least some, though I guess Kathy read me most of it when we'd hang out sometimes on weekends back up on the hill between the junior high and Old Trinity. We weren't boyfriend and girlfriend or anything, though some kids and maybe even some parents thought that. She was just the one regular kid I could trust and she was nice. We never became boyfriend – girlfriend either, except one night on the beach by Harbor House at the beginning of ninth grade. We both needed to try things out and there we both were, but nothing got changed by that. We were still just friends.

I'm convinced though that carrying a book meant something. Anyway, I was trying.

At the beginning of the summer after fourth grade they sold all the stuff from the Home Ec room. I know this because I went with my father to Columbus School where they auctioned all the stoves and refrigerators from all the elementary Home Ec rooms in the city. My father paid nineteen dollars for a stove that he jammed into the back of our 1961 Rambler station wagon, brought home, and put in the kitchen.

A few weeks later, hanging out in the school driveway that led back to the sixth grade playground, me and Mark Herman talked to three construction workers who told us they were splitting up one big room upstairs into two rooms. Mark, who was not a Book Room kid, said, "One of those is your retard room, I'll bet you." I punched him in the face, made his nose bleed real bad, but he was right.

Part Six: What

Because there was no second floor over the first grade and kindergarten wing the upstairs at Trinity was an "L" not a "U." And because of the upper parts of the gym and auditorium one of those hallways only had rooms on one side; except, as I have sort of said, the Art Room. On the long two-sided hall – except for a couple of fourth grade rooms in the new wing – you were pretty much in fifth grade territory. The other hall had the sixth grade, except that there was one sixth grade room, Mrs. Simon's class, on the fifth grade side of the corner. The Library was in the middle of the fifth grade hall, but next to it, where the Home Ec room had been were now those two rooms. Closest to the Shore Road and the corner was Mrs. Kelly; and the other room now had an official title: Resource Room.

I would divide my time between the two. Kathy had been right about one thing. The drool room – which had moved into a second grade classroom next to the cafeteria – was mostly for kids we had never seen before. They came in the morning on a short school bus or were lowered in their wheelchairs from the sides of Chevy Vans or Ford Econolines. They had people to help them eat; half of them couldn't seem to talk. Almost all of us from the Book Room ended up in the Resource Room.

And Kathy was wrong about the other thing. It was not OK.

First, there was this: I have said that there was a community in the Book Room and this was true. But it was a community of nods and heys when one crossed paths either in the doorway of the Book Room, or in the halls, or on the playground. It was a community of shared knowledge and experience and persecution. But it was not a community which had lived together before. The Book Room had served a diverse group. There were the retards like me who were called, "minimally brain damaged," the term back then for what is now usually called dyslexia. Then retards like Freddy Bonstein and Marty Tedder who never could figure out what would happen, "If you have two apples and you take one apple away." There were head bangers like Jimmy Silver and kids like Bobby Murphy who went crazy if anyone touched them – who just started screaming if anyone asked them too many questions. Then there were kids like Stevie Castelli who were just plain crazy. Stevie had stabbed his third grade teacher with her own scissors. He had probably beat-up a quarter of all the kids in his grade and the three below.

I'm sure the teachers called the result a "zoo." The regular kids, when not calling it "the retard room," sometimes said "the cage." Whatever the name it was very scary. There were usually at least two adults there at any time, including the lady from the Book Room, but there was no control. Bobby would be in one corner, screaming. Laura Ann DiMento in another, crying. Stevie would be running around hitting everyone. Jimmy and Billy Pellon would be literally banging their heads against the wall. Joey and Tommy would be jumping, I mean this, from desk-to-desk. Carol Conine never came out from under a table and when you passed by her she would curse at you. I'm sure the adults would say that they were teaching us in there, that they were helping us, that they were working with us. They probably were trying to do all three, but only one thing was really going on in the Resource Room. Anyone there that could was trying to protect their sanity – by whatever means possible. For the adults the solution was probably self-delusion. For those of us kids who could, the solution was to try to get out for however long we could. So though Mrs. Kelly's class was awful and she was a horrible person, I couldn't wait to get out of the Resource Room and get to a place where I would just get called "stupid" every ten minutes.

That sounds like Mrs. Kelly was picking on me. She was, but I really was not being singled out. She picked on everyone who wasn't a girl and a perfect student with perfect behavior. If you weren't all of these things, Mrs. Kelly had it in for you. Here are some examples: If you talked when you shouldn't she would draw a circle on the blackboard and make you stand with your nose in the circle for a half an hour. If your hair wasn't perfectly combed, like if you were coming back from lunch or recess and you had been playing, and if you were a boy, she would put one of those clip-on ribbons in your hair. A pink ribbon. Just to embarrass you. If you had dirt on you, she would tell you that you "should be wearing diapers." If she called on you and you didn't know an answer she would just say something like, "You are really stupid. I should send you back to second grade."

When I messed up, first, she'd do what she could to humiliate me, then she'd send me back to the Resource Room. I'd just go back and forth.

There were only these breaks: art and gym and music – all of those were OK. I'd get in trouble in gym, sure, but all that would happen was that Mr. Kelleher would make me run laps, around the gym or the playground, and I never minded running. And in art I'd be told to sit down a lot, but I always would. I just needed to be reminded and nothing bad happened. In band the trumpet occupied both my hands and my mouth. I guess I was too busy to do much wrong.

And there was also the AV room. This had begun in fourth grade when my teacher had needed, as I've told you would happen, to get me out of the room. Since she was nice, she found things for me to do in the AV room instead of just sending me to the office. Mr. Schmuckmin wouldn't let me bring projectors to classrooms – that would have been asking for disaster. But he let me rewind movies and set up the projector in the GP room and by fifth grade even fix broken film by splicing it back together. It was quiet in the AV room and I could do all this and be OK.

And there were the trips to the Book Room, which had changed again. The sign still said "SPECIAL SERVICES," but now it was just the people who wanted to "talk" to you about "what was going on," and how you could be "making better decisions." These conversations were more or less stupid, but they were also harmless. And I wasn't in Mrs. Kelly's room or the Resource Room.

All this led me to a new strategy. If gym or art or music was coming up, it was important to do everything I could to not get into trouble so I could go. If those weren't on the schedule, I'd try to get permission to go to the AV room. If that didn't work then the goal was to do something weird, something that would get you sent on a "special pass" to the Book Room. Of course I didn't figure this out all at once. It took months, til after Christmas, but once the plan was in place I was proud of it. It was the best way I had figured out to defend myself.

Bobby Murphy though had no way to defend himself. Most of the rest of us did. We had our strategies and if those didn't work, we at least had our anger. But all Bobby could do was cringe and scream. I don't think he could even cry. So when it fell apart for Bobby there was nothing. And it had to fall apart for Bobby, because you could barely have invented a worse place for Bobby Murphy to be if you had planned to torture him.

I would like to say we fought for him or that we tried to help. That would make us heroic. We would have risen above our environment. And I suppose we could have. We should have. Some of us had known him since kindergarten. He had been in my first grade class. I had watched him on the chairs in the office in second grade. He had even been in my fourth grade class mostly hiding in the back, but sometimes not. We knew that if you just gave him enough space and enough time, he could be OK. He wasn't a dumb kid really. He could amaze you with what he knew – if you listened to him, and stood far enough away, and didn't interrupt, and he was having a good day. We all knew this.

And at least some of us knew exactly what was happening. I knew – all fall I had seen him getting worse and worse. You could just watch the pressure build. He made himself into a smaller and smaller ball and packed himself tighter and tighter into the corner. His screams didn't get louder but somehow they got more scary. I watched and I did nothing, no one did. I could make excuses now – I'm sure a good child psychologist could give a good explanation, but that really doesn't matter. The fact is that I was, all of us were, just thinking of ourselves. When we saw what was happening to Bobby we were just happy it wasn't us.

Maybe me even more than others. When Bobby could do nothing but cringe in the corner, I understood this because I knew about that from second grade. When Bobby screamed when anybody touched him – I understood the fear even though I could manage my reactions better. I knew and because of that, I have never been sure that I am not as guilty as the adults who must also have known.

In the second week of January they took Bobby out of the Resource Room. I was in the hall coming out of the Boys' Room and I saw them. There were three adults including Mr. Kelleher and one other man I did not know. They were carrying him, and thus they were touching him all over the place, which obviously, you just couldn't do to Bobby. He was screaming, just screaming – a kind of howl that would scare the crap out of you if it was in a movie. The man I didn't know looked at me and snapped, "Get back into your classroom!" but I didn't go. I just stood there as they carried him to the stairs and the howl went on and on.

They took Bobby to the only place in the school that was worse for him than the Resource Room. They took him to the drool room. We knew that right away. Stevie Castelli came back from the office and he had seen them carry Bobby there. He told me this and then punched me in the stomach.

I've tried to imagine what happened next. I have to imagine this, because no one who knew anything ever said anything to any of us kids. No explanation was ever even overheard. So I've worked on it in my head. I started by trying to picture Bobby's brain and how it was different from mine. My brain seems like this: You know those Fisher-Price popcorn poppers that little kids have? The ones that you push and the little colored balls bounce around inside the plastic dome. Put ten times as many balls in there and make them all different sizes and maybe different shapes, and that's the inside of my head. It's chaos and a lot of times it is way too much for me, and I get crazy, but other times it's just the way it is and though it seems to bother other people it's not as big a deal to me.

Bobby's brain worked differently. He also had way too much coming in. I thought of his brain as being like part of that candy factory *I Love Lucy* episode. The one where Lucy and Ethel go to work and there's this conveyor belt and the candies are coming along and they're supposed to put them in boxes or something, and the conveyor starts going faster and faster, and they can't do what they're supposed to with the candies, and it turns into a big mess, and it's funny because it's TV and it's Lucy, but for Bobby it wasn't funny. I think things kept coming at him and he needed, really needed, there to be time for him to take each thing, and look at it, and decide what to do with it and put it on the right shelf in his brain – but the world just didn't give him enough time. So things kept piling up and crashing and falling over, and he couldn't get control over anything – it was just too much for him. Too many things could come at Bobby even when he was standing quietly over by the fence on the playground. Classrooms were way worse than that. The Resource Room must have been unbelievable.

And then they put him in the drool room, where nobody knew him and he didn't know anybody, and people were probably touching him all the time or at least getting too close, and who knows what kind of stuff was going on in there. It must have been like that conveyor belt doubled in speed again. It must have pushed him to the point where even cringing and screaming didn't work and he had, as I said, no other way to defend himself.

Two weeks later I was in the art room. I was by the windows looking down at the Shore Road. It was snowing. It had just started but was already coming down pretty good. Lots of kids were by the window even though the teacher kept telling us to sit down. It doesn't snow that much in New York so it's pretty exciting.

Bobby came running into our view from the driveway that went back to the sixth grade playground. We all knew him right away by the way he ran – his arms and legs kind of flapping wildly. He must have just bolted through the door the drool room had to the outside. It probably wasn't locked. You're not supposed to lock school doors from the inside because of fire. I imagine he was balled up in a corner and it was all way too much. He may have looked up and seen the snow and maybe the snow seemed calm and quiet to him. It does to me. And maybe he just had to get out into it. And once he was out, well, if I was Bobby I would've run too. Nobody had a better reason.

So we saw him run. It took only seconds, four, no more than five, from the time he first came into view. He crossed the parking lot and kept going. He ran onto the Shore Road. A mail truck swerved and jammed on its brakes. The teacher heard that and started running toward the window. Then a Rambler Marlin, a blue Rambler Marlin going the other way, hit him. It must have been going really fast. Even through the closed windows we heard it hit Bobby. It was loud. He flew through the air and just fell to the ground and all sorts of cars came skidding to a stop – their brakes and tires screeching – and the teacher got to the window and saw it and screamed and ran out yelling.

The street became full of people. Two teachers from the drool room came running from where Bobby had come. The art teacher ran across the parking lot with the band teacher. Mr. Schmuckmin came out with the school nurse chasing after him. Mr. Kelleher and the girls' gym teacher both appeared from the other end of the building. And dozens of drivers were out of their cars and we couldn't see Bobby anymore. But I needed to see. I had to see. So I ran out of the room and down the stairs and out the door into the snow.

Sirens were wailing in the distance and coming closer. The grass on the hill was already all white, the parking lot was almost white, and the parked cars were covered, but the street looked mostly wet. The people surrounding Bobby were all talking and together made a buzzing sound, like all the insects in the swamp on a summer night. I ran to the edge of the sidewalk and then slowed down. From the edge of Mr. Schmuck-min's wall I picked up a loose rock, though I don't know why, then I walked into the street. A police car with its red light flashing was just turning from Church Street. I went around the mail truck. I looked at the Rambler. A skidding Plymouth had hit it trying to stop and the back fender was all crushed. I had to walk around both cars to get to where Bobby was. Nobody seemed to notice me. They were all looking at Bobby or at the snow. Now an ambulance came from Church Street and police cars were coming from both directions on the Shore Road.

I slid around the front of the Rambler, slipping past the legs of all the grown-ups, and there Bobby was. Even with all of the people around him, I could see his face and I could see his blood. The only time I had seen anyone killed was when Lee Harvey Oswald got shot by Jack Ruby. But that was on TV. It was in black and white. And I didn't know Lee Harvey Oswald. I really didn't know that Bobby was dead but I could guess. There was a lot of blood. No one was trying to get him to breathe by blowing air into his mouth.

This was too late to try and be a hero, but I had to do something. So I screamed, "You put him in the drool room and look what you did to him!" and I yelled, "It's not fair, look what you did to him!" All the adults turned and looked at me as if I was the strangest thing they had ever seen, and the band teacher ran from where he was standing by Bobby and picked me up. I struggled, but he was much bigger and stronger. He carried me toward the school's front doors. As we moved under the concrete canopy I made my last gesture. I still had the rock in my hand. I threw it as hard as I could at the school. It smashed off the ceramic locomotive on the wall. The band teacher stopped for a moment but said nothing. Then he carried me to the Book Room.

Most kids never see their "permanent records" from school. For most, they are not very interesting. For most, despite all the threats that "this is going to be in your permanent record," I bet they're not very big either. Probably just a collection of old report cards and vaccination records, still sitting in some musty file cabinet in the basement of some old school or administration building, waiting for however long it is before they can be thrown out.

But I have seen mine. It is different. First, it is more than ten inches thick. I told you – the papers pile up. And it is filled with all of those tests and papers, even some of those drawings. The paper with the cut out car names from magazines is there and samples of my writing, year-by-year. There is the police report from when I punched a teacher in ninth grade and the referral to the "Alternative High School" that followed. There is the first report written by the rose-smelling lady saying that I, "demonstrate evidence of both minimal brain damage and hyperkinesis, which are likely to create permanent handicaps." There is also the report by a school psychologist written two weeks after Bobby Murphy was killed by the Rambler Marlin or by the drool room, whichever represents your point-of-view.

The term "Post-Traumatic Stress Disorder" had not been invented then and the psychologist spent numerous pages trying to describe it. He needed to add this to my diagnosis, but clearly, the general term of the time for the problem, the leftover from World War II, "battle fatigue," didn't sound right. He said that the traumas I experienced had, "seemingly overwhelmed the somewhat limited intellectual capabilities," and that this was, "particularly problematic in view of this student's immature social skills and significant behavioral problems." "Seeing a classmate killed," he went on, "would be a significant enough traumatic event for any child. In this case, however, it has exacerbated the long-term traumatic impact of violence in the home." This, he concluded, had led me, "to deep feelings of guilt and shame which are being repressed and converted to anger directed at the school which is being blamed for all of his problems."

It goes on. An entire page is filled with possible solutions that might work if I was not otherwise so "significantly handicapped." A long section details my "ambivalent feelings" towards my father. He makes much of my statements that, "Anyone should have seen what was happening to Bobby." He asserts that these are the "troubled imaginings" of "a boy unhappy with the world as it is." He ends by recommending "intensive psychotherapy," but then says, "Chances of success for this course of action seem limited."

I had talked to him for less than two hours the day after Bobby died. I had never seen him before. Stevie Castelli said he worked at the junior high in the North End of town where the kids were rich.

I found these reports because, after some things that happened when I was a cop, a police department doctor suggested that I go see a psychiatrist. I went because when something like this is suggested you really have no choice, but I wasn't planning to be very cooperative. The first time I saw the psychiatrist he asked me about "childhood traumas" and I said I didn't remember any. At the end of the session he suggested that I "search my memory" before I came back. So I considered messing with him. I drove to the City Hall in New Rochelle, which is where the Board of Education is, and asked if my school records still existed and if I could have them. My un-considered plan had been to drop a whole pile of papers in the psychologist's lap and challenge him to figure me out.

I didn't do that. First, they told me that I could see the file, and that, with enough notice they could make copies of the file, but that I couldn't just take it. That slowed me down. Then I saw the file, saw exactly how big it was, and I knew I would never hand that over to any employer, especially not a police department.

Instead, I sat down at a table in the City Hall basement and started looking through this record. I came back seven times over the next three weeks staring at the pieces of this personal history. I had them make copies of a few things – The first brain damage report. Something I had written in fourth grade about space travel with not a word legible – but I really liked the pictures I had drawn. The report card with the only "A" I ever received, from my ninth grade English teacher who told me that I could be a writer. And the report about Bobby. I keep these in a small, flat box that also holds my high school diploma and my diploma from the New York City Police Academy and the university degree I received more than twenty years after leaving high school. That last item seems to gain immensely from its proximity to these fragments of ancient history.

Bobby's death did not go un-noticed. In the months that followed, the Resource Room filled with social workers and student teachers and psychology professors and students from the college. It often seemed like there were more adults than kids. I suppose that in some ways all this made things better, but it is impossible to know. At home my mother blamed my father "for all of this," and when he was home their fights got even worse and now I really didn't fit under the bed, so I would sneak out and sleep in the dugouts they were building at the Little League field where Old Trinity had been, and then I'd sneak back in the morning. At school, two professors from the college made me their project – I guess now that I was actually their thesis – and they talked to me for hours in the Book Room. Mrs. Kelly now referred to me as, "just a waste of everyone's time," but Mr. Schmuckmin let me spend more time in the AV room, and taught me how to use the big reel-to-reel tape recorder and how I could even tape things from the radio.

The year went on. Then it ended and sixth grade arrived. The school did right by me. I had Mr. Garrett who was the only male classroom teacher in the school. He played football with us every recess, and he let me have a desk in the back of the room away from everyone else. He never sent me to the Resource Room except when it was "reading group" time and all the kids switched teachers. Mr. Garrett's room was the last on the sixth grade hallway. If you went down the stairs next to his room, you came out between the nurse's office and the first grade wing. I had completed the whole route.

I still went to the Book Room to see the social worker at least twice a week. I still avoided lunch at home and still slept in the dugout at times, but I did other things too. I made the All-City Elementary Band and I had a part in the sixth grade play. I won a ten-dollar bet by swimming from Hudson Park beach out to one of the islands in the bay, but the kids who bet me never paid. I went to my first boy-girl parties though some girls' parents really didn't want me in their homes because I was "one of those kids." I kissed Cindy Harrison. I went to one last Mets game with my brother, the day before he left to go to Vietnam. I gave up trying to learn to write cursive or print the small letters and decided to just stick to printing capitals, which is pretty much all I still do. Concentrating on one thing like that helped. Mr. Garrett even got me on the Safety Patrol; he thought that the responsibility would do me good. But that didn't work out.

Toward the end of sixth grade they made me take all the tests again. I knew from the other kids that this was about what to do with me in junior high, but they couldn't scare me anymore. I mean, what else could they do? I must have done OK anyway, because eventually they called me into the Book Room and told me that they would let me take "mostly" regular classes, but of course they would be "keeping an eye on me" and that I'd have to see the social worker every week. That was the last time I was in that room. The day I got told this Joey Mostone gave me my first joint and we got high in the gazebo at Hudson Park, overlooking the beach.

So the next fall I went to Isaac E. Young Junior High School and in seventh grade I told my English teacher to "fuck off," because she was asking too many questions, and I was in trouble from then on. And in eighth grade my science teacher told me that I'd pass for the year if I never went to his class. He said the same thing to Denny Belmonte. Denny knew that the little grocery store on Locust Avenue would sell anybody beer, and he lived right near there, so on his way to school in the morning he would buy a six-pack of Pabst Blue Ribbon or Knickerbocker. He would hide it behind a tree up on the hill above the tennis courts, and during third period, we would go out there and have three beers each – which made the rest of the day seem more OK. Once in a while Stevie Castelli would cut his class and have a beer with us, but he was still too crazy and it was better if he didn't. And by the time I was a junior at New Rochelle High School I had made a commitment that I would never walk into the school in the morning without being high, and I stuck to that. And through it all, I kept seeing lots of counselors and going to resource rooms and went to the "Alternative High School," which was in the same building but let you make your own schedule and do things your own way. All that, combined with the "self-medication," made life a little better and I graduated. And in the summers, as I said, I worked for the Parks Department and ended up going back to Trinity School, adding to the days I spent there, though by then, almost all the people had changed.

Later, I met other people and discovered other things. This has continued. I left and then, this day, I came back.

And as I stared at the Shore Road, at the brick building, Mr. Schmuckmin's wall, and the aluminum letters – I remembered another day when I was a cop. I had gone into a bar near New Rochelle Harbor called, "The Barge." It was after I had worked a four-to-midnight tour. I sat at the bar and ended up talking to a guy who turned out to be a New Rochelle cop. An hour later, I discovered that he was a cousin of Bobby Murphy. Before last call, I knew that Bobby Murphy was buried in a cemetery near the Kensico Dam, further up in Westchester County.

Now I needed to go there. And so I drove the length of New Rochelle – past Isaac E. Young, Main Street, the railroad bridge, the high school and dozens of other remembered scenes. Then up the parkways, on the way passing the cemetery where my grandparents, and father, and brother are buried. I drove around the base of the dam. I could remember a day long ago – I must have been very young – when I had stood near here with Mike and my dad on a hot summer day and watched the aeration field, ten thousand jets shooting the water supply into the air and into the sun before it dropped into the pipes that headed toward the city.

That memory began to fade as the snow began to fall. I suppose that it had to.

With white flakes beginning to swirl it took me more than an hour to find the grave, and by then the winter sun was almost gone. The head-stone read:

Robert Cullen Murphy
PAX HUIC DOMUI
March 2, 1955 – January 27, 1966

It was so peaceful here, under a bare old maple, just below the crest of the hill. The snow sliced the colors away, leaving only a calming few. The storm was creating a blanket of silence. I stood there and considered the fact that at our very best we still do only what we can, given the circumstances. And here we were again together in this place. A place, perhaps, where he might have been comfortable.

Hurricane

The storm is definitely coming and as the hurricane has races up the Atlantic seaboard we race to Dudley's and Hudson Park. The beers are frigid cold because the ice has been packed in for the expected loss of power and we suck green bottles empty as we push through the wind to the sea wall, already awash with each wave that tops the surge that rides above the incoming tide. The five most adventurous of us surf this suddenly violent water, wrapped in the shiny sea-mammal black of wet suits, as we cheer and drink and dance in the bright yellow of foul weather gear.

An hour passes and the hurricane multiplies itself. Our voices are lost in the wind's howl; our footing is lost in the deep green surf that now ebbs only between waists and knees. We cannot both drink and grasp the railings, so we retreat to Dudley's. There the water swirls ankle high and the Molsons and Mooseheads go rapidly. We place bets on the high water mark, noting, before we are reduced to the light of oil lamps, the carved marks of storms past.

At one in the morning the water covers our knees, at three it has drained back through the floor. A crust of salt is everywhere. We drift back to the seawall in the now dull rain, drunk on alcohol and Mother Nature.

In the park a fifty-foot sailing yacht, its stern inscribed with the name of a port twenty miles away, lies against a tree, impossibly far above the waters. We climb aboard, climb the rigging, and wait for the sun to arrive beneath growling clouds.

Bad Game

You would'a had to be in the locker room to understand how bad this was gonna be. You would'a had to.

We were playing at Mamaroneck. In that big old gym. We weren't of course "4A" New Rochelle High School. We were this weird little "single A" split off from NRHS. The retard school as everybody called it. "Alternative Education," as our teachers said. We played on the fringe — against other schools like us, including SITS in Mamaroneck, which might have stood for "School Inside The School," and little Catholic and Lutheran and Jewish and even prep schools. Along with "Sigma," the same kind of school in White Plains, we were the bad kids in this little conference. The image was grubby poor kids, which wasn't really true at all, but that was the image — and in our own way worked hard to live down to it, if you understand. Teams didn't like us, and sure 'nough, we didn't like them either.

We were the "Inclusion and Independence School," the "I's." And we didn't get to be purple and blue and white like NRHS teams, but were this weird Gold and Black combination that might have meant something, but I didn't understand. We didn't really have a name, so *The Evening Standard* started calling us "The Eyes," as in "Panthers Leave Eyes Blinking." Fuck them, but it stuck.

And really, we weren't so bad. Actually, we were good. At least my junior year we were really good. We could play with the NRHS JV, and these were guys who were gonna play real big time big city basketball the next year. Like have to play against guys who would climb out of Mount Vernon High School, or those big guns down in Manhattan, and eventually see the NBA. The varsity, sure, would beat the hell out of us, but we were athletes. I swam for the "regular" high school team, Chris played on their soccer team, Tiger did something like rowing, and we weren't the best here at all. Funny, the three of us all seemed totally different with those teams than we were here. I know I sure did. And that was more than just being buried in the silence of the chlorine water there and being surrounded by chaos here, or, maybe those were the things…

So anyway, we were in Mamaroneck. Rich kids. Assholes. Expensive warm-up suits. All these damn parents in suits and stuff sneering at us. Of course, we were in our locker room. Well, a locker room, I don't think it was the girls. No, it had urinals. Just a game locker room. At the smaller schools we used the girls' locker room and we'd write all kinds of great obscene shit on the walls and jam notes into the lockers. Normal adolescent boy stuff.

We weren't a good pre-game team. Dave, our coach, was no great disciplinarian, and hell, I'm not sure the school even paid him to coach us. He wouldn't usually even be in there until just before we came out, and he wasn't now.

Jenny *was* there, with me. Back in a corner of the showers. I probably just had a jock on and she had her shirt off and I was sucking on her tits and she was playing with me and I was rock hard and ready to just say "fuck it" and bang her right there on the scummy old floor. But then Mad Dog came in. Really Rudy, but he was just Mad Dog that year. My partner in the second string backcourt. The number two number one guard. Mad Dog held out a sheet of paper with lines of coke on it and handed me a rolled up dollar. Then he pointed to my hard on and said, "Nice look Head," which is what I was, either "Dope Head" or "Head Case," but it all came out as "Head." Then to Jenny, "Nice to see those titties girl." And Jenny said, "You gonna get him coked up then tell me I ain't got time to fuck him – I'm out'a here." And she pulled her sweatshirt on, grabbed her bra from the floor, reached over and grabbed my balls really hard and stuck her tongue almost down my throat. And I said, "Don't spill this shit." And she said, "Hey Mad Dog, don't you blow him before I do." And she stormed out and slammed the door. Then I did the lines, pulled my shorts on, and hoped the hard-on would drop off pretty quick.

I wandered out into the lockers with Mad Dog, and I think this is so different from the swimming team. When we get ready in those spaces off the pool, everybody is quiet. Some are just sitting on the benches naked – thinking, meditating, whatever. Some are wrapped in sweats stretching. Some are taking endless hot showers. Some are even reading. Yeah, people might be getting a little high, but it's all hushed, and nothing like what's happening here.

Cause here, shit is goin' on everywhere. Back in one row, Willie's shooting up. That's not a good sign. Listen. Smack's the dream drug sure as shit, but just the same, it ain't for playin' b-ball. And Willie, the number one two guard, is getting whacked by this habit. In eighth grade man, he could run and shoot with anybody on any playground we went to. I mean anybody. Back then, Willie could elevate over big guys and shoot the damn lights out. Anywhere. But now, well shit, in this league Willie can still score thirty a game playing just half. But he can't run no more, and he can't jump most of the time neither. A nigger who can't jump? Might as well be a damn white boy from Indiana, or me for that matter, who comes in whenever Willie can't breathe or gets sick. This happens a lot.

And ya know at least Mad Dog and me are doing drugs that wake you the fuck up.

Then there's Chris and Little Pete, who we usually call "Jewboy," and Nik, and Joe who is our starting point guard. They're all by this little open window thinking the smell is going outside, smoking weed. And there's Tiger, the power forward, slopping up multiple Nestlé's Crunch bars and yelling at all of them to "cut that shit out." Which is right. Don't get no weed buzz before playing b-ball. It's fine for swimming, but in the glare of the gym lights, it kind'a shuts your eyes. And that ain't good.

Big Pete holds court in the middle of the room, surrounded by the little sophomores and JayJay and BabyFat who split the small forward spot. Pete thinks we're all fucking drugged out losers who he's carrying. Maybe so. He's six-foot-seven and good. Drives a Trans-Am. Might get to play in college. But then, if he's carrying us, we could do whatever we want. Of course now he comes up to me, puts one hand around my throat and says, "You gonna ball that little slut fine, but not in here jerk off. Don't be bringing that little cunt in here; she ain't worthy of seeing my dick." To which I respond by smacking him on the ear, then breaking lose and nailing him in the gut so he crashes into the locker, and then we roll on the floor wrestling until Dave suddenly walks in and screams, "What the fuck are you assholes doing now?"

A legitimate question.

Dave pulls us together as much as he can, though Willie is sort of in dream-land now, and says, "We're going to press these rich little fuckers til they panic." He looks at Willie and tells me it looks like I'm starting and to not be "your typical loser fuckup boy." He sends BabyFat to the food stand to get coffee for Willie. He starts to say something inspirational. Fuck, ya know, we've won six in a row now, he ought to. But we've gotten him into the spirit, and he just says, "Oh shit, get the fuck out there," and we go.

Big Pete and Tiger want this team stretch, which we sort'a do, and then to warm up off the weave. But right off Chris and Nik collide and fall down on the floor laughing and the damn Mamaroneck assholes are laughing at us, so we just start shooting. I'm way outside, which is really the only place I can shoot from because I'm a midget who's got no jump. And I'm sort of talking to Joe who's off at the edge of the court making out with Annie. Jenny looks at me and yells, I mean yells, "Hey Head, are Mad Dog's blow jobs better than mine?" And Mad Dog just turns around from under the basket and wings the ball at her, and misses, of course, nailing our math teacher in the head. Sweet.

So Dave grabs me and Joe and says, kind of growling, that he's gonna personally ram a baseball bat up each of our assholes if we don't cut it out, "Now!"

The game starts. We jump out ahead. Joe gets three quick fastbreaks, Big Pete two or three jams. I think I get two jumpers, both off steals. We're up by ten in no time. Cool. Then we start to blow up. No, we're not going to lose this game to these little cocksuckers. We're way better than them. But we start to blow up anyway.

Still in the first quarter – Joe gets called for traveling. Joe goes ballistic. The ref calls a technical. I get in Joe's face and say, "Shut the fuck up, not home refs. Shut the fuck up." But he doesn't. He says, "Get your scrambled fucking Head out of my way." Then he kind of climbs over me and tries to hit the ref. So he's out. Dave kind of carries him off the court, but he's still screaming. We end up with five technicals. Five, man. But that little jerk off one guard of theirs only makes two. Screw it.

Mad Dog comes in. And for a while, we seem OK. Then Willie comes in for me to start the second quarter, and Willie goes wild. Scores a dozen fuckin points in, damn, I don't know, five minutes. Now we're up by like twenty. So we're cruising. Even little Pete gets in the game instead of JayJay and BabyFat. Big Pete nails this awesome rebound, and I'm watching this, with my hand pressed right in Jenny's cunt cause she's sitting right behind the bench, and fires it out to Willie who's as far back as he ever gets on defense – ten feet the other side of half-court, and Willie takes it, strolls in and nails this awesome slam, then just falls on the floor and passes out.

The Mamaroneck coach and doctor are freaked the fuck out, but Dave knows what's up and just has us carry him back to the bench. So, I'm back. "If there was one damn brain in this backcourt," Dave says, "we'd be dangerous." Then, in his fatherly way with me: "Don't fuck up."

We get to half time. Up by twenty-five. No one cares at all now. Mad Dog and I skip out on Dave's little pep talk to go smoke a couple of cigarettes, and do a couple more lines. "Stay awake motherfucker," Mad Dog says to me. "Stay the fuck awake." But when Mad Dog heads to take a piss, I find Jenny, grab two beers out of her backpack, and slam 'em both. Need to be level. Too much coke. I push open some side door of the building and piss out onto the step. Jenny tells me I'm one real gentleman.

Back to the game. Now I'm having real problems seeing, but I'm just shooting. Just chucking. Cool. Some are falling. On the rest, Big Pete and Tiger are getting the rebounds and putting 'em in. No one cares, but Dave is screaming. Then the next crash. Mad Dog drives the lane. He always walks when he does that, but he always get away with it. But this time he crashes into their big guy and gets flipped into the air – for a moment he's totally upside down – and hits the floor with a noise that echoes in the gym, and I mean, you hear his fucking leg break. You hear it.

They get the stretcher. But everyone knows better than to take him to the hospital right now. Dave decides to let him watch the rest of the game. Sitting there with Annie's old man who's kinda like our team doctor. Also the city's medical examiner. We're probably the only live patients he's got. Everybody hopes Mad Dog looks a little less like a speed freak in an hour when he does get to the hospital.

Now me and Chris. But Chris is a pure shooter, really a pure chucker. So now, I'm the damn one guard, which really sucks because I'm not fast, and I'm getting sick as shit, and the Mamaroneck coach thinks he's going to get back in the game by pressing me. OK, good plan. But I'm still sort of functioning, and I get Tiger to come back with me to take the inbounds pass and then bang people out of the way, so I can get loose. And we're not losing much ground. But during the foul shots, I'm going over and drooling in the water fountain.

Five minutes left when this dipshit forward comes into the game for them and tries to guard me. He thinks he's slick. He says, "You stupid little drugged out guinea. You're smelling up my damn gym." Fuck him. I ain't no guinea. So I do what anybody would do. I stop. I take the ball and fire it into the bleachers. I get right up to him so I can scream the fuck at him, but instead I puke all over his pretty uniform. He's looking at me. He's just frozen and looking at me like I'm the lowest kind of scum. Off in the corner Mad Dog is just howling. And then I punch the asshole right in the fucking mouth and now he's covered with puke and blood. I get jumped by like four of them and it's a motherfucking riot.

We finish the game playing the only four guys who didn't get thrown out. But we still win by like ten. Fuck them. They suspend me from school for a couple of days and from the team for the next game. Fuck you all. Cause, sure, I'm back in school in plenty of time to be at the next swim meet, where, high on nothing more than weed, I come in first in the two-hundred. Like when I got suspended the year before for throwing the water jug into the bleachers and hitting the damn superintendent's daughter. Still, back in time to swim against White Plains. So fuck everybody, we all know the game. Mad Dog has to spend like four days in the hospital. The police come to talk to him twice but nothing happens. Willie scored forty-eight points in the game I missed. After I get done puking the rest of my guts out, Jenny and me smoke weed and fuck all night on a mattress on the floor of Joe's basement. We have breakfast with his parents. I take her to breakfast again at the diner during first period. She's cool. I know her dad would like to blow my fuckin' head off.

At the end of the season, we make the regional championship game and lose to other rich kids from upstate in a big college arena. The coach from the college looks at us, sneers, "Get those fucking hippies off my court," and then stomps away.

My parents tell me I'll end up dead or in jail, ain't sure which they're hoping for. *The Evening Standard* calls us "The Red Eyes." Real, fucking cute. My mother says I better damn well get to confession, but I don't go. Ain't been since I was ten. Though I lie about it.

It's like Mad Dog always says: "You know, mother's just half a word." He says it that night. He says it two years later at Willie's funeral.

Shelter

Frieda and Bob had this huge, fantastic house, way the hell out on Shelter Island, which you can only get to by ferry, and amazingly, because this was unlike any other rich people I knew, it was always open and they were happy to have us use it whether they were there or not.

They weren't usually there because they really lived in Brooklyn in another huge house, an easy commute for Bob who worked for a law firm at Rockefeller Center, but the key was under the mat and the 1961 Ford Falcon Futura wagon with what remained of red paint was in the driveway — if you needed to get to the grocery store for more than you could carry.

It was July, and Joe and I both skipped lifeguarding for the week and rode our bikes the eighty miles, maybe more, from the end of the subway in Queens. We wanted Walter, Frieda and Bob's kid, to meet us, but he said no, so it was just us. We finally got there and collapsed on the couches in the music room that overlooked the bay with a great curve of windows and slept and slept and slept.

Waking up it was afternoon and pouring rain. We grabbed foul weather jackets off the hooks by the kitchen door, left the bikes and the Falcon, walked the mile down to the only real bar on the island, and drank beers and played pool, with the Rolling Stones on the jukebox.

Going back up the bluff Joe says, "I think she's pregnant." I say, "No shit." He says, "I got no fucking idea what to do." I say, "You could marry the bitch or the two of us could just hit the road and disappear and not come back." He says, "Don't call her a bitch." I say, "Sorry." He says, "You got that scholarship, you ain't gonna blow that." And I say, "Jesus fucking Christ."

At the house, we throw everything we're wearing in the dryer, smoke a joint, and find beds. The next day it's still raining and we wish Kyle or Eddy were here and could play the Steinway grand in the music room, but they're not. So we go to the beach and swim all day – who cares if it's raining if you're under water?

Two days later, it hasn't stopped raining and we've thrown all of our clothes in the dryer half a dozen times. Somewhere between the house and the bar, we almost talk about putting the bikes in the back of the Falcon and driving home. But I just say, "You know, maybe she isn't." That night I dream of sex with a girl whose face I cannot see and wake up sticky.

On Thursday, Frieda arrives and explodes into the role of mom and cooks deep, dense food, and plays Mozart after dinner as the day ends across the bay. She asks how we are – and maybe because she's not our parent and barely even knows our parents, and hasn't lived in our town for six years – she's a safe adult, and we tell her. We start small with my panic, and only hours later in the light of an oil lamp on the porch, get to Melissa.

She listens. She says, "Whatever you need Joe. You know Max and I can help." She says to me, "Get over it kid. Get out to that place where nobody knows you and just be whoever you can be right now." Then,

"But call or write or something, and, you know where the key is." She goes inside and plays a Rachmaninoff prelude and we follow her and fall asleep on the couches with the notes loosening the fears.

On Saturday, we ride the other way, the wind fighting against us, the sun finally present, searing our bare backs.

Hawkins Street Ends at the Water

Timeline

It started raining *Thursday*, which was our first day back on four-to-twelves. *Friday*, when it was really only drizzling, he got killed. Then the days went like this: *Saturday* I got interviewed all day by the detectives from the Borough and from Major Case. *Sunday* I got drunk and never left the house. *Monday* I went to the wake in uniform. *Tuesday* I went to the wake, but not in uniform, dragging a very reluctant Carolyn. The funeral was *Wednesday*, and it was still raining. *Thursday* should have been the start of the next set of four-to-twelves, but they had me listed on the sick report; so while Carolyn was at work I went up to the Mall in New Rochelle and wandered around after I had lunch at Dudley's. *Friday* I rode the subway all the way downtown in the morning and saw the shrink as part of this new "crisis intervention" crap they've got going. As if they really care. But hell, he wrote out a slip giving me the rest of the week off. He held that slip and just as I was reaching for it said, "Two more things." And I said, "What?" and he said, "First, I'm going to guess that you're right. That you are a pretty good cop. And you like the job; you're telling the truth about that." There was nothing to say to this so I didn't say anything. Then he said, "Second, you also know that what you said at the beginning doesn't matter." And I said, "What?" again. "It doesn't matter that you weren't friends," he'd said. And he let me take the paper from him.

So anyway, I don't have to be back at work til Thursday night, eleven thirty. He should've gotten me out of the week of midnights. God, I hate midnights.

Well, we weren't really friends. We weren't friends at all. We're now linked by this event and people want us to have been friends, because that would make the story play better, but it isn't true. We'd known each other long enough: the same company in the academy, the same rookie unit, the same precinct, the same squad – to know that we pretty much wanted nothing to do with each other.

In fact, our last words were maybe fifteen minutes before, when I said, "Hey asshole, thanks for taking off just when we're getting busy." And he told me to go fuck myself.

Pinball

The sign over the storefront simply says "TAVERN" alongside a rusting and faded Rheingold logo that surely pre-dates all of the customers tonight, except for the three guys playing cribbage at the table by the front door, who are probably into at least their sixth pitcher. On the front window, there's an artistically painted "Bay Street Bar" sign that, along with the placement of daisies in empty green Molson's bottles on each table, attempts to lure upscale tourists during the summer. But to everyone here it's simply "Amo's" named after an owner few of us remember. And since it's October the tourists and the daisies are gone, and most of the small crowd has walked here through the misting rain on this amazingly warm night.

"You should join the Y," Carolyn says to me, "You can join the one in New Rochelle can't you?" I mumble an, "I guess," in response. "You need a place to swim when it's cold. You should do that."

She's in an amazingly good mood. This is cool. I'm drinking as fast as I can to catch up, because she's being totally hot and sexy. Right now, she's got her leg stretched out under the table with her foot rubbing my crotch, and I need to take advantage of this. "Yeah," she finishes this line of thought, "I think you get a little weird without time in the pool."

I say that I think she may be right. I agree that it's a strange thing for me not to swim every day, after doing it for so long. In the summer of course I can just dive off the rocks by the house and crawl forever through Long Island Sound, but that would be a mighty cold plunge right now, no matter how warm the air. "Maybe," she says, "it's just that you spend too much time wearing clothes these days." And she laughs and gives me a look that is the kind of pure lust a couple married less than a year should share every day.

I tell her that I guess a bulletproof vest isn't as big a turn-on as a Speedo. She says, "No matter how ugly a Speedo is." "I thought the uniform might get you hot," I add, because I think it did for a while, but it's not very true anymore and she just lets this drop. "I'll play you pinball for your clothes," she says. "Cool," I say, "I'm much better at pinball than you'll ever be." "Then I want odds," she says. "No problem," I say, "What odds?" She looks at me, "One piece of clothing per ball, but your socks and shoes don't count." "Then I'm only wearing three things," I say. "Good," she says, "this'll be quick." She pulls her foot away from me, gets up, and walks over to the very old "Fireball" game in the corner.

We need this. It's certainly been a weird week or so. I watch her dropping the quarters into the game and begin to count back, running through this week's timeline, trying to do it without considering the events as anything other than beats in a measure. For the moment this works.

She starts to play and I get up and walk over to the bar to get two more beers. I think that she's probably right about me needing a pool. It's not that I miss the constant smell of chlorine on me or the battle against crotch rot from wearing tight nylon. I don't think I miss the competition either. Who's going to miss finishing seventh? But, yeah, I need something.

I walk up behind her at the game and kiss the back of her neck. I notice that she's playing way better than she should be. "Get off me," she says, "I'm winning here." So I lean against the wall, look out across the bar, and try to escape for the moment out of The Bronx. I believe I can do this because I've prepped myself for it, walking here tonight without my gun or my shield, not even my NYPD ID card, and so, skating on all that cop-type responsibility thing. And we're back playing strip games in public, which we did heavily back in Michigan. We'd play strip anything: poker, backgammon, cribbage, pinball, Monopoly once – though that was confusing – air hockey, foosball, whatever. Not that we often actually took our clothes off in those places. Well sometimes, but that's a college town and you can get away with shit like that there. Mostly we'd pay off back at one house or the other. But obviously, it was always good foreplay no matter who won. It will be tonight.

Plus, I think I like this place. It looks just like all the bars I grew up in, but people only sort of, maybe, know me. We've only been here, well, not quite a year. And this has been mostly either winter, and we stayed inside, or summer, with the island overwhelmed by visitors and everyone anonymous. So I have no history here, which I suspect is good, even though we're only a few miles from where I grew up; even better, maybe only two or three people here right now are sure they know what I do for a living, no matter what's gone on recently. Though one of those is Byron who's tending bar, and who might think I'd do something if some nut job walked in with a gun to stick the place up.

Carolyn's won a free ball and is playing that and she says, "I'm taking your pants on this one." "You ain't won shit yet," I say, and wonder what's making her so happy because if I've been weird the last week, well so has she. And I've got reasons. But then if I've got reasons maybe she has reasons. And maybe yesterday being kind of like the end of it all, maybe I'm ready to stop being weird and maybe she is too. At least that's what I'm thinking as the ball finally falls between the flippers on her and it's my turn. "Beat that," she laughs.

I shoot the ball into play before I'm really ready and though I surely don't want to I'm thinking for the moment about yesterday morning, and that shrink the department sent me to, and what a waste of time that was. I guess it was. And because I'm thinking about that, I let the night with Sean creep into my head: part of that first image – the wet sidewalk, him lying there, the guy in the Georgetown jacket running down the street, slides almost softly into the reaches of my peripheral vision. As the ball is careening down from the top bumpers I have to shake my head to clear it. I reach for my beer instead of the flipper button and the ball escapes. I drain the beer.

"Wow," Carolyn says, "you just wanna be naked," which starts to bring me out of it. Then, "Should I take these now?" she says, sticking her hand in my back pocket, "or wait til I've got everything?" Byron walks by on his way to the back cooler and plunks two more Molsons down for us. Carolyn tells him she's beating me in strip pinball and is it OK if I get naked in here. He just laughs and says he doesn't think they have the right license for me to dance on the bar, but maybe that only applies if I get tips, and he doubts I'll get tips.

She's right. I know that. I need a pool and chlorine. I need a specific pace of breathing. I need the blurred view that comes with immersion in liquid. Water – that's always been the healer for me. When stuff's been crazy, and it has been no doubt, the silence of the water has always worked. You can't hear anybody, you can't see anybody, gravity almost stops, and you get down to only two essentials, moving forward and getting oxygen. The rest of the world vanishes. And so you come out clean in the end. Really clean. Whether the dirt is all the joints you smoked, or other drugs you did, or how badly school, or home, or even all the other games you end up playing, you can send it all down toward the drains, and you can come out clean. Maybe even now.

She's playing this ball really well too and I look at her and think she's pretty fucking beautiful. I think, well, damn, this has really been a pretty good year, overall. I graduated from the academy. I know people thought I'd never manage that, but I did. I'd been great in the academy. "You did exceptionally well in the academy," the shrink had told me yesterday, though he added the inevitable, "especially considering. . . ." I had wanted to say, "Fuck you" to him because I had done exceptionally well "not even considering." I finished second out of seventeen hundred cadets. What else did I need to prove? So I didn't think at that point it was necessary to bring up the fact that I was one of those "scholarship" guys, a white guy who benefited from the attempt to hire more minorities through free tutoring for the civil service test and extra help with the academy class work. Because I mean, obviously, except that there are still plenty of people, and Sean that asshole, was one of those, who think I'm a retard who did better than I should have. Anyway, when the shrink said, "especially considering," I finished his thought, "considering I'm a retard, right?" and told him that Sean was one of those same jerks, which is just one reason why I didn't like him when we were together in Company Thirty-Three and why I didn't like him in the rookie unit and why I didn't like him in the second squad in the Four-Seven – so maybe why it's not the world's biggest deal to me that he's dead. I said all that. I needed to clear up the misconception that this was all somehow devastating or something. It's not.

I mean, yeah, it's one more of the bad stories, but there are more good ones than bad, you know, and that's as much as you can hope for. I thought about this yesterday taking the subway downtown to the shrink's office. I took the Pelham Bay line down instead of one of the trains from my precinct because, well, I don't know, it's my "home" train – the one I rode every day to the academy, the first subway line I discovered and jumped the turnstiles of when I was a kid. It's familiar, really, that's all. So I took it yesterday and I realized I was scanning the other passengers, looking at them in a way I didn't use to check out subway riders. Not really looking at faces much, that's too obvious, but checking hands and wondering what might be in pockets, in waistbands, in that paper bag. That's what training does – it's become my norm. That's all right. It's what I do. This is what my friends don't understand. How cool a thing that is. The people on the train were safer because I was there. If something happened, I could have done something about it. Would have. I have the gun, the skills, the authority even. The decision tonight – to not be in that position of responsibility – *that* is doing something different. Most of the time, almost all the time, in or out of uniform, whether people know I'm there or not, I'm making people safer. I'm actually making their lives better.

I think, isn't that amazing. And I know that I'm pretty proud of being a New York Cop, cause we do that. It's not as if we're annoying assholes that give people tickets for five miles over the speed limit or parking at an expired meter. We're actually kind of super-heroish. People are happy to see us. Maybe we're the only place in America where people are always genuinely happy to see a cop.

Looking back at Carolyn I also think of her, and being married, which hasn't always been easy I know, but still, it's good. And the house we have where Hawkins Street dead ends into the water, which is old and drafty and desperately needs paint we can't really afford, but is awesome anyway. It's just three blocks from here and amazingly – it's on a dirt road, and there aren't many of those in The Bronx, not even on this strange little island.

So things are good, except that the way she's playing now I'm gonna have to kick some ass to get back into this game, but when it's my turn she starts putting her hands all over me, messing with my head, and she won't stop no matter what I say, until I finally let the ball drop and complain that this really isn't fair and she just says, "You're down to your t-shirt, babe," and grabs my balls before she shifts her attention back to the game.

I need to take a leak so I slip around the corner to the men's room and after I piss, I find myself kind of staring into the mirror while I wash my hands and splash water on my face. The light is so much harsher in here, the bar being really pretty dark, and it reminds me of, oh shit, yeah – I see the picture that defined the whole thing with me and Sean. The picture in the *Daily News* with me standing in the Jacobi Emergency Room in my underwear, pouring peroxide onto my uniform to get the blood out. There'd been plenty of other pictures: Sean's crying fiancée, his neighborhood gathered around his house in the rain, the one from academy graduation day with the three generations of cops – of course all the funeral scenes, made, I'm certain more poignant by that steady drizzle that soaked everything. But the shot of me, that had become the one. Shit, some stringer had gotten famous. Of course, the whole thing in the papers was so damn absurd: "Cradling the bloody head of his fallen comrade he both directs the search for the assailants and pleads for the paramedics to get there," the *News* said, making it sound like a black and white World War II movie with violins on the soundtrack. On the Op-Ed Page of the *Times,* it played more as a fragment of a Vietnam film: "In the aftermath of one more senseless act of urban violence, on a dark side street washed by a cold October rain, one rookie cop desperately tries to keep another alive. His voice on the 9-1-1 tapes showing that strange mixture of professionalism bred from intense training and human desperation." Neither is recognizable to me, I'd told the shrink that. I said, "It wasn't like it sounded in the papers."

I don't even really remember talking into the radio; I mean I guess I did. Colin had chased down the street with the car – I'd jumped out. What I do remember is trying to stick Sean's brains back into his head. As if that was going to work. But it was all I could do. He was dead already, and so I just knelt there on the sidewalk in the rain holding onto his head, his blood pouring all over me. It soaked completely through the uniform; my underwear was stained dark red. At the hospital I found little chunks of brain stuck all over my clothes.

"That's not the first time I've had to do that," I told the shrink to calm him down, "we all do that all the time."

"Really?"

"Oh come on, my first day out of the academy I got covered with somebody's blood." I said to him. "I work in The Bronx not in Midtown. People are always getting shot or stabbed or just cut. There's blood all over the place." There was. That's one of the things that's surprised me, how much blood I've run across: victims' blood, blood from accidents, the blood of perps, my own blood even. You strip and pour the peroxide over your clothes and scrub your hands and arms and face with that hospital soap and later you go home and you stand in the shower for as long as the hot water holds out.

"Does that get depressing?" he asked.

"Nah," I say, cause no matter how obviously true this is it needs to be denied.

"Does it matter whose blood it is?"

"Well I guess it bothers me most if it's mine," I say. I tell that old joke to try to break off the discussion.

Now I throw more cold water on my face to get out of this line of thinking. And I notice that my hair is probably shorter than it's usually been at this point in the calendar, before the first meet of the seasons, and after just letting it grow since the March before. It's surely much darker too without the endless sun of a summer spent lifeguarding. I surely tried to get as much lay-out time as I could in this year, and probably my hair's pretty long as uniformed cops' hair goes, but still, am I almost looking adult?

There's a strange thought. I dry my hands and face and push back out of the fluorescent brightness into the dim of the bar.

Carolyn's sitting on a bar stool next to the pinball machine with her head leaning back against the old wood paneling. "Where you been?" she wonders. I say I was taking a leak and start playing while she taunts me. "You are gonna lose boy," she says over and over, establishing a rhythm that works incredibly well as a distraction. So I'm just thinking fuck it, ya know, either way we're gonna race home and get it on. So, with the ball bouncing around at the top, I take another long hit on my beer and watch the spinning disk in the middle of the game. That's the trick to this game, playing the ball as it comes off that disk. Now the ball falls into play and I begin to control it. I'm doing fine – I mean I'm a pretty damn good pinball player, back at school I was almost a wizard, but my head cannot stay with it tonight and long before I'm close to what Carolyn's scored, the ball falls down the tube.

She's just getting crazy and funny and we're gonna play out the last two balls in the game. This only lets things build. I ask what she's playing for now and she smiles and says, "Don't worry, I'll think of something."

I'm thinking of too many things, that's for sure. Obviously, I'm feeling impending sex and that's making me nuts, and at the same time all her talk about swimming has me almost smelling chlorine. Then there's everything from the week, like I'm catching glimpses of the funeral in the reflections in the beer ad mirrors, and in between the dings of the pinball machine and whatever's on the jukebox, I'm hearing bits of radio crosstalk and bagpipes playing *Danny Boy* and chunks of yesterday's conversation with the psychiatrist. Anyway, all these things are flickering on the edges of my senses, and I'm getting overwhelmed.

Albany

My junior year I had only qualified for state as part of the relay, and we did really badly. The coach tried me as the anchor, but I'm not the one you really want finishing the race. I can't do that. It's just not my style.

My senior year was different. I was the star. I still wasn't good anchoring either relay. Jed did that. But going third I would build our lead and Jed would hold it perfectly. So going up to the championship weekend in Albany in March – I was there for the hundred, the two-hundred, the four-by-one-hundred, and the four-by-two-hundred. It was big time. I already had the scholarship, of course, and I could talk like a big guy cause I was going to be a Big Ten swimmer the next year.

We weren't really in Albany. We were near Albany, on a campus with a real pool. One that was fifty meters instead of twenty-five, which means you only turn half as many times, and means you only kick off the wall of the pool half as many times, which means you have to swim a lot more. And, well – only swimmers understand this – swimming is the slowest thing you do in a swimming race.

The fastest thing is the falling. The gravity and momentum on your entry dive is the fastest you're going to go. You take that as far as you can until simply, you need air, and only then start the arm stroke that brings you to oxygen. The next fastest is at the end of your turn, when you've flipped and are halfway through the twist that re-orients your body, and your legs kick you off the wall. If I knew physics I could probably explain this better, but I know it's true even though I'm not sure why. Anyway, the swimming part, the stroke that pulls you through the water, mostly with your arms, that's the slow part, the part where you're just trying not to lose much ground. That's because the acts of pulling yourself through the water, and of course breathing, pulls you out of the fish-like form you can create while gliding and into the resistance-creating form of a land animal trying not to drown.

We got there two days before – a huge thing for our high school to do for us, the coach kept telling us that in case we'd missed the point – just so we could get practice time in this new environment. This was good, but not nearly enough, because you have to refigure all your strokes and when to start turns and all that. At the end of the first day there I was tired and missed the count, and wasn't looking I suppose, and swam smack into the wall at the end of the pool, lucky not to crack my head open.

"Thank God you're fast," the coach told me, "cause really, you're almost too stupid to swim." I thought that was enough, but he went on, "and that's mighty stupid indeed."

When the whole thing started, there were hundreds of swimmers from all over the state, swarming around anonymously in gray sweats, except for a few kids from Long Island and the guys from Scarsdale who had warm-ups in their school colors. And because this was swimming and not a sport anyone pays any attention to, you really have no idea about anybody, though rumors and stories do spread. So every race is pretty much a surprise. At least in the prelims.

I assume I'm invisible, although at one point I overhear two guys talking about, "A kid from New Rochelle in the two-hundred who's got a scholarship to Michigan State." But then the second voice said, "Michigan State? Screw that, it's not like it's Indiana or something."

But screw them, because I won my first heat in the two-hundred. Actually, I blew away my first heat in the two-hundred. And the two-hundred relay won its first too. I qualified in the one-hundred, then the one-hundred relay – we won that heat. At the end of a day and a half of qualifying, I was still in everything.

Later that day I found myself out under a tree getting high with three people I didn't know. I didn't get high when I was going to swim. That was some kind of personal rule. I did get high to play soccer. I got very high to play basketball. But I didn't for baseball and I didn't for swimming. After, sure, but not before. I don't know the reasons.

This was after. And there was one guy from Buffalo named Daniel, and one guy named Matt from Rockland County who I'd seen at meets before, and one Onondaga Indian from near Syracuse who was named John – but whose last name I couldn't really get my tongue around. Matt and John were actually the kind of almost famous you can be when newspapers write about minor sports. John, because he had this huge cheering section from the Iroquois reservation and thus the Syracuse paper had sent somebody to write about him. "Indians invented the crawl," he'd said, though I actually have no idea whether that is true or not. Matt, because his dad had died last year, and the suburban papers had given him this big write-up before the championship. New Rochelle's newspaper was part of the same chain, and so carried the story. One of my basketball teammates showed it to me. When I'd wondered why there wasn't an article about me, he said, "They usually don't write about retards."

We got really high and we talked for a long time. John came from a town that had been the capital of the Iroquois for more than a thousand years. "That's awesome," I said, meaning it absolutely. Daniel was somehow French-Canadian. He had gone to elementary school in

Montreal, but his dad worked for GM and they'd moved across the border. He still had the accent. Matt didn't say much. I asked far more questions than I answered. These were exotic tales I had in front of me – people with histories and communities, with attachments stretching far out of my field of vision. I couldn't offer them anything like that.

Matt's dad hadn't really died. Well, he had really died, of course, but he'd been killed. This was in that article. He was one of two cops in Harlem who got ambushed as they got out of their car at a fake call. They thought they were going to something like a baby-getting-born call, and bam, some guys with rifles on the roof shot them. It was very big news and I guess that I remembered it from when it happened. But I didn't like cops. Not that I'd had any real bad experiences with them. In fact, they'd mostly been OK, all in all. Just that winter I'd been driving down Main Street with three of my friends, getting high, and this cop had stopped us. But he didn't bust us. He simply looked at me and asked, "Do you really think this is the best place for that?" And then he let us go. That was pretty cool, actually. But I wasn't the kind of person who'd like cops. And I wasn't really the kind of person who read the news deeply. So it wasn't a very big story for me then.

I'm not exactly sure how this story leaked into the conversation that afternoon, but it did. And when it did we were all pretty silent until John told us how – in the very old days – when babies died, the Iroquois would bury them under intersections of the forest pathways, so that their souls could slip into new babies when pregnant women passed by.

When we were all completely wasted, we walked across the campus and down the street to a Burger King, and goofed around and wore the crowns they give away.

The next day I swam the very best time of my life to get into the two-hundred finals. Four fucking tenths of a second better than I'd ever done. Absolutely incredible. I knew during the race that it was happening. The water was just parting for me. But I didn't really know until I saw the results on the board. Then I saw my dad up in the stands. My dad had actually shown up there. He'd been traveling and I hadn't even known that he knew that this event was going on.

Naked

The thing of it, I think, looking across the bar again while Carolyn plays her fifth ball, is that Sean was no random thing. He put himself into that place. He was on his way home for God's sake. He had things to do. A woman to be with. And he stops to play the hero. All by himself with his stupid little five-shot off-duty piece, he's going to break up a robbery? He had no business there. He had no idea what was going on. He never saw the second guy. The guy who just coolly stepped out and blew his head apart as he ran by.

If he had just driven past. Just gone on home to his pre-wedding party or whatever it was. It would have been one more report. I would have gladly written the report. The detectives would have happily handled it. His fiancée would be OK. His parents and grandparents would be OK. The neighborhood where he grew up would be OK. The city would be OK – just one more anonymous robbery in the northeast Bronx. And I...well, the week would've been different.

I told the shrink this yesterday. "He shouldn't of been there. He shouldn't of stopped. He was off. He should'a gone home."

"Cops always say that," he said. "Tell me, if you saw a robbery on your way home, you'd just keep going?"

"I don't know, I guess it depends." I said, but I know it doesn't. This job, it doesn't ever stop. And that's not just because of the rules. The rules, which go way back to when Teddy Roosevelt was Police Commissioner, say you're a cop twenty-four hours a day, seven days a week. You are always supposed to have your gun with you. You're always supposed to act. But I don't think it's the rules that really matter.

Just a month ago, I was driving to work when my car broke down in the little town that borders the precinct up along the Sound. I walked up to the Post Road to call work and tell someone to come and get me. As I was walking toward a pay phone this car jumped the curb next to me. It wasn't going fast though. I looked and the driver was passed out. So I ran, as fast as I possibly could, got along side it, opened the door, and jumped on the brake. Then I pulled the guy out. He wasn't breathing, and I started CPR.

In a couple of minutes, the Pelham Manor cops arrived. Then the ambulance. They said I saved this guy's life. They tried to make me sound like a hero. All I wanted was a ride to work and for them not to tow my car away from where I'd left it, in front of some rich guy's house. Eventually they got me to work. They even got someone to fix the fuel pump in the car. They gave the local newspaper this big story about what I had done. The guys I work with thought differently. "You're an asshole," Marty had said, "You're jumping into a moving car like you're some kind of stunt man? You get run over or your ass dragged along for a mile and you'd of looked pretty stupid." "Yeah," Tim added, "You're off-duty, you're not even in the city. Who cares if some old fuck dies of a heart attack?" Sean had said, "Doesn't sound like you. Were you high or something?"

"Depends on what?" the shrink asked.

"Depends on whether I think or not," I said. "I guess if I think then I ain't doing nothing, but you don't always think." This is probably true. The only thing is, you never think, you just do. It has taken me awhile to realize this. When I first got hired, they "swore us in." This should have been dramatic, but it was not. We did it all together, standing up in a high school auditorium on that first day, in between filling out the tax forms and signing endless sheets of city employee paperwork. Almost two thousand of us mumbling meaningless words. Except they turn out not to be meaningless. Somehow, we agreed, either during this oath or at some point that our lives were less important than the health or safety of anyone who lives in or works in or happens to wander through the City of New York.

And, staring for a moment through the bar's front door – I wonder: no gun, no shield, but, what would I do if things went bad right now?

When I left the psychiatrist's office I got into the elevator. I didn't want other people to be in there but other people were in there. Maybe six. All women. All Manhattan-dressed New York women. The kind of women who would never be in my precinct. Who would only be on my island on a summer Saturday after *The New York Times* Living Section announces, *"Top Ten Surprising Places, Right in the City."* If they even saw me, I'm sure I was mistaken for a delivery guy. If they had seen the gun they'd of been terrified. I thought I could let them see the gun. But I didn't. I didn't do anything. I just stood there staring at my smeared reflection in the aluminum doors until they opened on the lobby.

They all got out while I waited. They didn't know I was a hero who made them safer. Am I even sure they would've cared if they'd known?

Carolyn breaks this thought. "C'mon boy," she says, "I think you're playing for something big here," and she points to the score totals shining behind the machine's glass.

It doesn't matter. Of course she's won. So I just play until I lose, not putting much into it. My brain is drifting too many places. When I'm done, she hooks a finger into one of my belt loops and pulls me around the corner.

"Now," she says, and starts pulling my shirt off as she backs through the door of the ladies' room. "*Strip.*" She makes this a command. "I want my winnings now loser boy." I look around, then think, fuck it, and kick off my sneakers and drop my pants. She can tell I'm ready, no matter how distracted I might seem. "Gimme," she says, holding out her hand, and I step out of my pants and pick them up and hand them to her.

She throws my clothes in the corner and grabs me and kisses me, totally intensely. And within a minute, her pants are off too and we're at it. Wildly, insanely, noisily. Who gives a fuck? This is great. Great, but, what can I say? Quick too. Of course. But that's OK, we'll get back to the house, we'll do it again. More for her.

I wrap myself around her, and in that momentary aftershock, find myself staring at the floor.

And the floor in the ladies' room is different from the men's, or maybe it's just cleaner and so more noticeable. It's that pattern of little hexagonal black and white tiles like those old hallways in all those old apartment buildings. I remember this book my friends bought me back when I first told them I wanted to be a cop. It was called *Police Work*, or something like that. It was filled with black and white photographs of cops on the job, mostly in scenes that were scary, or disgusting, or simply exhausting. "Your old friends," they had written inside, "present your new ones." Part of a months-long campaign to talk me out of this crazy idea. But I kind of liked the book. It showed something that looked really real to me. I especially liked one picture: A lone cop stood in a grimy tenement stairwell, the floor patterned in little hexagonal black and white tiles, his gun pointed at someone out of the frame. And the caption said something about how, when he worked nights, he wondered who was watching out for his family. Then it said, "It made him diligent."

Carolyn starts pulling her pants back on. I think about that picture. About Carolyn at home on nights when I'm working. About what I do. About heroes and stupidity. About promises. About how Sean, who thought I was a lazy, sloppy retard and who I thought was a brown-nosing asshole, would understand completely – but this woman, my woman – who stands there in front of the mirror, her blond hair now wild from my hands, doesn't, won't, can't. About working crazy hours and different days and friends I don't see anymore. About funerals. About chlorine and how many strokes it is from one end of a pool to the other or how many strokes it might be from here to the lighthouse across the Sound at Execution Rocks, and about how I don't even need the fingers on one hand to count the number of races I won after that day in Albany, my times getting better in college, but never again being good enough. About my father who worries about me without ever saying it. About my father who lived through being a hero in the Korean War, and his father who lived through being a hero in a war before that. About who might have held my brother's head that night in Vietnam. About kids I don't have yet. About the people I get to help, every once in a while, and how they say, "Thank you officer," as if I really count. All that. And then now about being naked in the ladies' room of this bar.

I reach for my clothes, but she moves with amazing speed and grabs them first. "No way," she says. "I won these." She opens the door and heads for the back entrance. I slowly peer out the door, judge that no one's looking my way, and quickly follow.

We push through the door and I'm naked in the alley under a surprisingly bright light. "C'mon," I say, but she's already jogging away, so I start after her. It's late. There are only a few lights on in the houses around, but there are porch lights, and lots of windows. So I start out nervous, but after I cross Fordham Street, excitement starts to take over. Then I discover that it's not raining anymore. I look up and the clouds are starting to break. A star or two shines in the night. Carolyn's almost a block ahead, where the alley meets our street, just laughing.

I run naked through this dark island, but really, not very fast. The air washes over my skin, warm, erotic, dangerous. When I turn onto Hawkins Street I see that the three women who live halfway down are drinking on their front porch. They will see me naked. Carolyn is yelling to them that they will see me naked. I don't care. They will see me naked.

I spend enough time in uniform. I've spent time in enough uniforms. They will see me and then I'll chase my wife the rest of the way home and we will make mad-hot-wicked love on the living room floor. We will fuck all night. We will be crazy. Tomorrow is Sunday and we will stay naked all day. Because I'm alive. I get to do that.

On Monday, I'll go up to New Rochelle and join the Y. On Thursday, around eleven-thirty, I'll go back to work.

Sundays

By nine-thirty I'd've climbed out of bed, showered in a hurry, pulled on jeans worn all week, gone out the window cause why bother, fired up the old Corvair that seemed to be running on just five cylinders, and wound my way north. Past Main Street on Church, up Memorial Highway, past Lincoln Park and the Projects and the old 7-up plant, twisting through streets, around back of the high school, finally to Maggie's.

She'd hear the mufflerless whine, bolt out her back door, slide in next to me, and we'd drive back down to the bar strip below Iona's campus, parking behind the pizza place that was, when I was a kid, a White Tower hamburger stand. We'd start walking. I'd smoke. She'd talk.

We'd roam the streets on either side of North Avenue til we found her dad's car. The Mazda he'd never let her drive if he wasn't passed out. Once we found it, we'd race downtown, the rotary engine squealing the tires at every light, to the diner where breakfast let the rest of the morning roll past.

But always back before he might wake, having picked up the Corvair, dropped the Mazda without comment. Maggie back beside me. Telling stories. Never about dads.

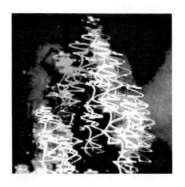

The Speed of Christmas Light

Home

There was no place else to go. It was freezing. We were all broke. At various houses, in various places, parents and families were missing for various reasons.

It started out with three of us. Josh and Meghan and me. Josh swam the two-hundred too, but faster. He was one of those too brilliant guys, majoring in Japanese and Agricultural Economics. Meghan did huge nudes as a painting student. They were really good. Lots were self-portraits but others included me and Josh. I did huge nudes on an art department Xerox machine. One of the people to crawl across the copy machine for me was Meghan, but there were many others. I called myself a graphic design major. This meant classes that really weren't classes, just studios that I could do well in. This meant I kept my eligibility. This meant I kept my scholarship and the ability to finish behind Josh in meets. Or to see it a better way, to be both creative and a legitimate part of the four-by-two-hundred relay.

Anyway, it was the three of us – five days before Christmas. We drove all the way west in Josh's 1971 AMC Gremlin into the Manistee National Forest along the Muskegon River and found a tree we obviously were not supposed to take and took it anyway. Tied it to the top of the Gremlin, which then had to be pushed a long way through the snow. Then we got insane drunk with Josh's old high school friends. We slept on someone's floor within sight of the ice forming on Lake Michigan, then drove back with our tree to the big house I lived in, right across the street from the totally empty campus.

Josh and I went out to buy lights at the Meijer Thrifty Acres. Meghan stayed at the house, wearing swim team sweatpants and a slightly too small paint splattered t-shirt that she looked incredible in, and baked Christmas cookies that would be the ornaments. At the store, we filled our cart with one hundred white lights, cat food and cat litter, rolling papers, totally obscene panties as a gift for Meghan, eggs and bacon and bread, toilet paper because that seemed essential, and four cases of beer. We met Caitlin who Josh knew from Japanese class, and then Andy who swam the four-hundred butterfly and whose parents were heading out of town – told her to make sweet potatoes and him to bring alcohol, "preferably something like champagne," – and invited them both. "Good champagne," I yelled, as we walked away.

Before we left we needed to wander the aisles looking at everything we couldn't afford. Well I couldn't. Josh probably could've if he'd asked his parents for cash, but he really never did. Thrifty's sold everything in the world or at least everything the consumers in a depressed Midwest capitol city might expect, so, food and clothes, toys and hunting rifles, and coffeemakers. Eventually we got to the bikes and Josh told me about getting this awesome Batman bicycle when he was ten. And then I told him about the Christmas when I was three or four.

Josh had grown up in this big house outside of Detroit and I bet Christmas was pretty spectacular, but you know, that really doesn't matter. When you're a kid Christmas just about anywhere is spectacular. So I explained how there was this enormous tree that glowed with all the magic of the world in colored lights and glass balls, and the long chain of paper links my sisters had made two days before. Did he know about decorations that poor kids have? Again, it didn't really matter. And I talked about the universal thing – it still being dark outside and slipping from the bedroom and staring, in that moment between amazement and greed. I told him how I knew there'd be crayons and paper, books for the girls, and one toy to be expected, not wrapped, because it would be from Santa.

"Santa wrapped our presents," he said. "Why would Santa wrap anything?" I asked. We were still standing by the bikes, and I went on because I had to tell him that then in the lights, I saw this amazing red and chrome tricycle that wasn't like any other tricycle, cause you pumped it with your arms to make it go and steered it with the pedals on the front wheel. No other kid had anything like it. And then I bounced onto it and burst out of the apartment and raced along the halls – screaming.

"Very cool," he said, meaning it. "Yeah," I answered. Later, maybe the next day, maybe four years after, I heard my dad ask, "How'd he know how it worked?" I just always wondered: How could you not?

We went through the checkout and loaded the stuff in my little FIAT, which never could get warm in this weather and slid through a snow squall back to my house, where we found that Meghan's cookies were mostly in the shape of male genitalia, which should have been expected, and that she had invited two other people she knew. So three days before Christmas we were at seven.

Forty

When Christopher is fourteen the tree is pretty much the same as it has been for his whole life, though ornaments have come and gone. Little electric candles still mark the windows. There is garland on the porch one more time. I'm still up long before my kid, who's now as tall as me, a better athlete, a math genius, an almost prodigy musician. So good at school stuff that he is more bored than anything else. Aren't genetics an amusing thing? But the house is different and the windows look toward a frozen, saltless, Midwestern sea a few blocks away. Maybe later we can go play out on the ice. There's a craziness to that. Just enough risk to make it great. The Big Lake doesn't freeze flat and solid, but in broken, jagged bergs, and the farther out you venture, the more gaps of open water you can find – the more dangerous it gets, the more fun.

Inside it's almost warm, as snow flashes past in quick, abrupt swirls, driven by the onshore wind. "Lake Effect," they call it – the cold wind blowing over the water, picking up moisture, and dumping it in great quantities as soon as the air reaches land. It's a trade off, of course. More snow, much more snow than even ten miles inland, but warmer in winter, cooler in summer. And snow's all right. Especially for Christmas.

The two of us. Though next year he'll be in high school. Then, just four years later, college. The thought of that makes me afraid. It does.

Of course, there've been other people. There've been women. Three, four, maybe six? Some at Christmas. Sure, it's nice at Christmas. I've worried about it being confusing for Christopher, but yeah, of course it's nice. But none have really stayed. It gets that way. None right now. That's OK. Maybe it won't be in a few years. Maybe not. But now, it's fine. He'll wake up in a while. Or, maybe I'll wake him. We'll open presents. We'll make breakfast. We'll listen to The Messiah. We'll watch old movies.

Hands wrapped around the mug, with good coffee from the kind of exotic places I've never seen, I stand in the living room and look at the tree. I've always wanted to go places, but it's never happened. Not even Europe – much less Africa and coffee plantations in Kenya. Never off the continent, except for Newfoundland once and of course Long Island, which obviously doesn't count. In the center of the tree is a crumbling wizard, glued together again this year, bought at Macy's in another life. A little below is the "Baby's First Christmas" carousel that lights up. Still there. And below that the presents. Almost all for Christopher, though I've bought and wrapped two things for myself, because, well, because.

Santa has been better this year than his budget should allow, but then, there is the pressure of limited time. And well, things are going to get better. It's been hard out here. Life in exile, as I sometimes describe it. Different jobs. Different things. But I'm almost through school now. Isn't that amazing? Actually doing more or less OK in a college. For real. And then I'll have actual "credentials." And maybe I can make real money again, that would be nice. But meanwhile, well, I've done a lot of extra work this fall. There's been money. So a new violin bow, which is the only thing he asked for. And the new Nintendo, because he didn't ask for that.

After presents and breakfast and movies we'll eat again. Something that looks like Christmas dinner, quick Turkey that I'll heat. But I'll fix it up. Cranberry sauce and maybe candied sweet potatoes. Those have sort of gone with Christmas forever I'm pretty sure. Anyway, something like that. Maybe less than four years you know. In just a couple, there could be a girlfriend, and her family for him to go to. There could be. That happens.

Night

By Christmas Eve, we were up to eleven, and Josh and I went back to Thrifty Acres and bought a gigantic turkey, and all sorts of other stuff that left us with a combined eleven dollars and seventeen cents to get us until our scholarship checks showed up at the beginning of January. But we figured there'd be bottles to return and maybe Meghan had some cash and we'd be all right.

We watched *Miracle on Thirty-Fourth Street* on channel fifty from Detroit, happy about having climbed the pole and rigged the illegal cable hookup back in September. I told stories of Macy's and the tree at Rockefeller Center and the moving window displays on Fifth Avenue to my Midwestern friends, making it seem like New York City was something I was personally responsible for. We got stoned and drunk and it felt much later than it was and Meghan talked about going to Midnight Mass but the snow kept coming, really hard now, and there was just no way.

One of my housemates had a big waterbed and so the three of us, and Roger, the ten-week-old kitten I had found in the art building, piled into it, and smothered ourselves in blankets and went to sleep. That room also had an aquarium, and we left that lighted, the soft warm blue fighting off the dark.

Sometime around two or three — I don't think there was a clock around — I dreamed something bad, swung one arm and hit Meghan. We both woke up, startled and confused. "What's going on?" she asked, reaching out to me, kind of kneading my shoulders. I told her I didn't know, but reached for a joint and lit it and we passed it back and forth.

"What's going on?" she asked again. And I said, "Thinking about Christmas." She said, "Not exactly sugarplums?" And I laughed. Then I told her about being thirteen, this time the age was clear.

On December twenty-fourth that year, my dad got mad and smashed my face in. I guess it was seven or eight o'clock and I had come home late, and things probably weren't going real well. He said something and I said something and he said something else, and I said, "Fuck you" and he nailed me, right under the eye and I bounced off a wall and was bleeding all over. This was in the little hall by the kitchen. Everybody else must have been in the kitchen or the living room. They didn't see.

I took off. I bolted out the door without another word, ran down the stairs and outside, then through the back routes I had known all my life, avoiding the streets so I could be alone. Across Main Street, I climbed the stairs to the top elevator lobby in the parking ramp of the new mall. I lay on the floor there, pressing my face against the cold tile, trying to keep it all from swelling up. I found two old tissues in my jacket pocket and held them to my skin, and eventually the blood clotted and dried.

As I said all this Meghan only stared at me, almost as she did when she drew or painted me. I looked down at myself and realized that in the dream or the awakening I had managed to shred the t-shirt and underwear I was wearing – that I was pretty much naked. But that didn't matter. Meghan and I knew each other's bodies absolutely intimately, without ever having shared a sexual touch. A year later she painted me at that moment from her memory, my body at the best it would ever be, polished by the pool, and still vaguely tan from a summer spent bartending nights and lifeguarding days, strung with just the remnants of cloth. Behind me, she painted snow and a clear starlit night instead of the room and the fish. It got her the top prize in our senior show. But that was later, at this moment she just stared, and I went on with the story.

I went to Midnight Mass that night. Walking all the way up to Holy Family halfway across town, where no one would know me, and I stayed way in the back and didn't take communion. Then I walked the other way, under all the Christmas lights stretched across North Avenue and Main Street and got to Kathy's house around two thirty, climbed up to her window, and banged on it til she looked up and let me in. She got a washcloth and band-aids and cleaned me up and we fell asleep in her bed. We didn't face each other, but she held on to me through the night.

When it was morning she went down to her Christmas tree. I went back out the window and with three bucks Kathy had lent me, bought cigarettes and a carton of orange juice and two Hostess pies, from the only store open. I walked to Hudson Park and went over the hill and down to the beach, over the rocks that are underwater at high tide and found a place out of the wind and curled up on the hard-packed sand.

I saw the tide come in, and go out. Then I saw it come in again. And when it finally retreated once more, I knew it was the twenty-sixth. Then, once I knew that, I climbed back over the rocks, went back through the park, and this time, walking in the middle of dark streets, I went home.

When I finished this it was quiet for a long time, just the fish tank's air filter and Josh's breathing. "Shit," she finally said, "that's a pretty…" but she didn't know what to say, so she stopped. "It was just a quiet Christmas," I said, "Maybe that's OK."

Then I added, "There were good Christmases." I said this defensively. "Yeah," she said, "Josh told me about the tricycle. He liked that story." "Me too," I said picking up the cat, which stretched and almost snarled on being awakened. We lay back down and slowly drifted back into sleep.

Morning

I wanted to start this morning with the Messiah, but I've switched to a cassette I recorded off the radio years ago. Harry Harrison – who used to do mornings on WABC, when it was the ultimate top forty rock-n-roll station in America, and now does mornings on "Oldies" WCBS-FM – did these hours and hours of Christmas pop tunes. Harry Harrison has woken me up more mornings than anyone else. And he is doing it today. I'm sure I'll get back to the Messiah at some point.

He hasn't actually woken me. I haven't slept. Not anticipation or anything. Just something I don't do much anymore. Sleep seems to bring too many things these days. Too many thoughts. Too many pictures. When I'm awake I can hold them at bay, my vision filled with other things. But at some moment, often just after that drop off into sleep, they come at me. It has become easier, maybe even healthier, to simply stay awake.

I pour coffee for myself. Look above the door to the kitchen clock. A wild 7-up advertising thing I stole from my high school as a graduation present to myself. It's pretty hard to tell time on, the hands have been bent and straightened and twisted and sort-of straightened again, but it's something after seven. Or a lot after seven, maybe closer to eight.

Christopher is not up yet because he is a weird kid. A cool kid, but weird. What percentages of four-year-olds sleep in on Christmas morning? Not a lot, I'm sure. So he's asleep, and I'm up. I suck through the coffee, despite how hot it is, and pour more. I walk to the living room window, to the scene that's there, a surprisingly violent surf and rain strafing the house.

More than six months? Yeah, more than six months. We've been alone here for more than half a year and it seems as though we've gotten used to that. But this is Christmas, so it's different. It will be different.

Generally, things look the same. Inside for sure. Outside there's still garland on the porch railings, but it lacks the obsessive wrapping of the pillars that Carolyn would demand, supervise, and criticize when on the first or second or third try it wasn't 'properly' spaced. I just had no reason. But in here the tree is in the same spot, decorated basically the same way. Christopher insisted. So it is. And that was easy because there's been no real property split. She pretty much left everything. Said she was on her way to a different life. Or was all of this just my way of holding on? Whichever, it is pretty much the same inside, as Christopher wants. This has been the pattern. I say that I want things to look different. To be different. For us to be out of the house. To be other places. Christopher the opposite. The same. Staying in. As it always was. A conflict I guess. For various reasons, he usually wins.

Under the tree there is too much: Yeah, overboard. But nothing from his mom. Nothing. Will she call? I don't know if that would be good or bad.

I wander back to the kitchen. Pour still more coffee. Caffeine and the lack of sleep make my hand shake and coffee splashes from my cup onto the black and white tiles of the floor. I drop a paper towel and wipe at the spill with my foot.

Now Harry Harrison talks about all the little things that should make you know it's a good year. "Waved at by a celebrity. Run to by a happy child." Two hands on the cup, I go back to the window. Beyond the breaking waves the Sound has vanished in the rain. It is just all gray.

Snow

In the morning, the town was totally buried in snow. One by one we got up. I made breakfast. Meghan stuffed the turkey. We gave her the panties and a t-shirt that said "Speedo" on the front and "Swimmers Do It In The Water" on the back and she modeled them for us. We started some other food and listened to the *White Album* and *Exile on Main Street*, the 1930s *A Christmas Carol* playing silently on the TV. The house filled with smells, turkey and stuffing and, of course, fresh cut pine. At one point, we all ran out, barely dressed as we were, and made a trinity of snow angels in the front yard.

Sometime after the second basting of the bird the doorbell rang. And oddly, it was Andy and his parents, who were supposed to fly out the night before, but who were now snowed in. Though we had never expected guests with adult status they were of course welcome. And they had brought good champagne. Actually, they brought great champagne. Then everybody else came. The food piled up and Andy's dad carved the turkey since none of the rest of us had ever done that before. We stretched the table to fit thirteen. "Biblical," I said to Meghan by the stove. "To Christmases yet to come," she said, "To better Christmases," and she raised a bowl full of gravy as a toast.

So, on that cold day in Michigan the party went on. We ate and ate and ate – drank a lot too. We told stories, probably self-censoring at first because of the adults, but then those rules faded away. This seemed to go on for hours until we were all too stuffed and drunk and we fell onto the furniture and rugs in the living room.

People talked about favorite Christmases, but I don't think I did. I might have brought up memories of food. One Christmas my uncle had appeared with dozens and dozens of fresh clams dug that morning and we ate them every way: raw, steamed, fried – a great feast. That was very exotic for my Midwestern audience. I might have even made it sound like it happened more than once.

We watched *White Christmas* together and then *Holiday Inn*, talking less and less as time went on. The snow still drifted down outside the windows. The fireplace, stoked with wood from the pile at the fraternity house down the block, warmed the room. All of us, I guess, were relentlessly comfortable in the moment.

Later, I went to the kitchen to get more champagne and found the cat spread eagle atop the turkey carcass, consuming what must have been more than his weight. I didn't say anything, not wanting either to disturb the cat or to make anyone worried about eating the leftovers.

After I got back and filled everyone's glasses we toasted Christmas one more time. I noticed Andy's mom fingering one of Meghan's tree ornament cookies. I froze for a moment, because I didn't want anything to wreck this day. Then she turned and looked at me. "Ooo, " she said, "candles."

First

Carolyn and Christopher still silent. I'm awake and padding nervously through the house. From the kitchen to the living room, over to the windows. Seeing the gray of the water, the sky, the distant edge of Long Island. Bumping the thermostat up a degree every five minutes until I'm comfortable in just torn, old jeans. Coffee made, and the beginnings of breakfast sizzling on the stove before the first startled waking sounds might come from the crib.

I looked at the ornament collection, the invention of our family holiday, the invention of traditions: wizards, gnomes, angels and such, made from glazed bread dough and cheap, all things considered, from "The Cellar" at Macy's up in New Rochelle. They joined the Hallmarks, the "First Christmas Together" we'd bought at the after-Christmas sale three days after the wedding, and now the "Baby's First Christmas," a carousel that lit up from grandma. I'd again insisted on a shaggy looking tree, one that looked like it came from the woods and not a farm. She'd driven me nuts through a whole day spent wrapping the porch railing in garland.

Last night, I'd spent hours carefully assembling his gifts under the tree. Needing to match the scene exactly as I'd drawn it for our Christmas card a month before. The last remnant of the art career. The blocks right here, the rocking horse to the right. The little wooden train set on the other side. The one that's way beyond anything he could comprehend, that I'd driven all the way past Kensico to some fancy upper Westchester kids' store to find. I had to get it. I'd drawn it for the card. And after drawing it and making all the copies I'd hand-colored the little train on each one we sent out. I know, pretty boring work from the guy who Xeroxed naked people. But a commitment. Art takes many forms. Anyway, it had been after three a.m. before I'd been satisfied.

Eventually, the cry came. Because I had nudged him? Maybe. Sleeping babies make me nervous. Are they breathing? At work too many are not, especially in those early morning hours at the end of midnight tours, and I do get scared. Carolyn would hear me coming home from a four-to-twelve – moving toward his room. "Get out of there! If you wake him up I'll kill you."

Now I go and lift him from his crib, change him as the cats look on. We'll go wake mom. He'll see the tree, his presents. There'll be pictures. Relatives will come by. We'll eat at grandma's later. Just like it's supposed to be. Yeah. Just like that.

Light

Almost two weeks went by. School started again. People back in town. Even a meet in West Lafayette and an unexpected night there when the weather turned vicious. Then the snow stopped though the temperature crashed into a cold almost unimaginable. But the stars came out. Meghan and me and Josh walked back toward her house from blowing too much money and busting training rules at a Twelfth Night dinner at a restaurant called Beggar's Banquet. We'd laughed and talked and drank for hours. Now, our faces wrapped in scarves, we moved through the arctic night silently, only the sound of our boots crunching on crisp snow.

The street was dark and halfway there Josh stopped, and Meghan and me noticed and stopped too. He pointed at the stars, then pulled the scarf from his mouth and told us about a spacecraft called Voyager that would be launched the next year. He said it would travel the length of the solar system, looking at all the planets – and keep going, way out into the next century. Way out, beyond the future. Out to a time when I'd have not heard from either of these friends for more than a decade.

I stared up, then moved my finger a little to the east. "Somewhere out there," I said, pointing at the vague glow of the Milky Way, "is light from a star that's almost two thousand years old. That sparked on the first Twelfth Night."

"Didn't you fail astronomy?" Josh asked. "Yeah," I said, as we both pulled wool back around our faces. And the three of us stood there for another minute or two, our faces to the endlessness of that night sky.

Rain

Joe and Mad Dog and Me and Chris. Still school year, but hot. Playing ball on the courts back behind the Junior High. Dark. Playing by the security lights. No one around but us and Maggie and Jenny and Bobbie and Annie. Maggie and Annie say it's gonna rain and so they've got these big umbrellas. I say no, just gonna be too humid and I wish I had a car that was air conditioned, but fuck, I'm lucky to have any car so shut me up.

We're playing in our jeans and it does start raining. It explodes raining. Tropical New York. Instantly it's pouring and lightning and everything. The girls are all under the umbrellas, but we're into the game.

But the jeans gotta go cause they're so heavy now we can hardly walk. Then Maggie says, you fucks should just play naked so we can compare. Me and Joe and Mad Dog throw our shorts at them, but Chris, he won't. The girls are just laughing but it don't matter. Me and Mad Dog are up, and we're gonna beat these guys all night long.

A Descent into the Maelstrom

You know, I guess if I could just shoot someone, blow them the fuck away, watch their damn body — no head, the head would be better — explode — see all that blood splatter, I might feel better.

Even better, I guess, if it was some damn woman. Not just any woman, but some angry female with maybe some similarities to Carolyn. Then I'd really feel better. I'm sure.

I know. Not for long. I'm not a violent person. I don't do real well in the aftermath, after I do get violent. It hurts for so long, and so bad. But it really might help right now.

And I do need help. I mean I'm out-of-control depressed these days. Hopeless, hopeless depressed. Worse. I know I'm totally depressed. Usually me knowing it means I'm on my way back up, but not this time. I've known it for weeks, but it doesn't matter. I keep spiraling downhill. Is the Paxil helping? I can't tell. Some people tell me I'm "looking better," but other people are treating me like I'm closer to the edge than ever. They look at me, and the gun I carry around all the time, and they don't like the combination, even if it wasn't a problem for them before.

It's two-thirty in the damn morning and it's hot as hell outside, but we've got the car air-conditioned down to maybe 55 degrees, cold. Not as cold as the old Plymouth Gran Furys could get, that Chrysler Corp "Max AC" setting still beats everything else, but it's been years since there were Gran Furys, so the Crown Vics have to do. Better cars. Bigger, handle better, more comfortable, come with FM radios. Everything fine except the AC was better in the old days. Still, we got it cold, which is one damn fine accomplishment when it's 94 degrees and humid as a Mississippi swamp up here in The Bronx.

The radio is squawking. Yeah, sure, I'm listening; I probably even know, if I had to, which I sure as hell don't, where all our cars are. Adam's down under the El by the park on a shooting, at least I know that. So I'm sure the boss is there to. Henry is, well, maybe I don't know. Right, I don't have to. We're up here by the mouth of the river. It's quiet here. If you don't let yourself see the abandoned cars and trash and shit, then you'd think this wasn't even The Bronx. All the cattails here. The Hutchinson River wide and flat as it spills through its swamp into Long Island Sound. If we opened the windows, which is not going to happen, we could hear frogs and geese and, yeah, plenty of mosquitoes. It's like out in the middle of nowhere, but the legends go that this is where they caught the guy who kidnapped Lindbergh's baby. Another century. But even here I guess we're in a place where we could get anywhere we're needed in a hurry. I guess. Just jump on US-1 or I-95 or even 233 and we could, if we were needed. Which we're not. And we plan not to be needed. "Four-seven special five," that's what we are, a designation signifying not a thing. Meaningless to the dispatcher. She won't call unless no one else at all is available.

Colin's being real quiet. He looks totally exhausted. Just chain smoking to stay awake. That's why I'm driving. I'm not sure he can see at all right now. We've got the tunes cranked up on the real radio – right now the Allman Brothers are playing – but then we've got our police radios cranked too so we can hear the jobs. Yeah, obviously I'm quiet too, at least externally. I'm not talking, but *obviously*, I'm thinking way too much.

But listen. I ain't crazy. No, I am not crazy. And no, I'm not gonna kill no one tonight. Not for no reason, and not for my own reasons either. Not tonight. Not tomorrow. Not never. I'm depressed, flipped out, way tired. Been one fuck of a bad month. But I'm a responsible guy. I don't do real stupid shit. I'm in control when I've got to be, and when I'm working I've got to be.

Don't believe me? What am I doing here at two-thirty a.m., two and a half hours after my shift ended, working in plain clothes in an unmarked car? Am I here cause the boss thinks I'm a looney toon? I don't think so. A sergeant doesn't come downstairs to the locker room and beg a cop he doesn't trust to work an extra four hours, covering for guys out sick. He's not gonna negotiate with someone he thinks is too crazy to have out on the street with a gun, just to get him to stay out on those streets. He sure ain't gonna say, "Sure, you don't have to change back into uniform," and "Sure, we'll get you an unmarked car," and "Sure, whatever else," if he doesn't think the cop is someone he can depend on. I'm someone he can depend on. Handle the calls. Do the right stuff out there. Not get into any shit that's not essential. He can depend on it. You can depend on it. No matter what any department shrink might think last week, this week, next week. Even right now – as all messed up as, yes, I admit I am – I'm the guy he can depend on.

The thoughts about blowing someone away? Yeah, they're there. So what? If everybody didn't have thoughts like this there wouldn't be any of those movies out there that fill every theater. You know, any of those movies with people getting blown away. Don't know why, but I guess that sometimes we need to see that. It's a fantasy, that's all. And no, I'm not gonna talk out loud about it. See, I ain't crazy.

Besides I have blown someone away before, remember. Well, it ain't nothing like those movies, or even this fantasy of mine. It's just totally ugly man. Don't ever think anything else. It does shit to you, changes your life, and that's not for the better. You give up this huge chunk of yourself, and you can't get it back. And for what? For what? That little stupid set of colors with the leaves on it that's over my shield. It's right there, on the leather backing with Shield #25013 that's hanging against my chest, inside my "State Swimming" T-shirt. Well, OK, there's the real whole medal sitting in a box, where is it? Probably stuck in the back of my underwear drawer. But that's it? Two pieces of colored steel in exchange for a big chunk of yourself that you give up for something that has not a damn fuckin' thing to do with you? Two pieces of steel and whatever the hell it is we get paid, which is nothing if you're trying to live anywhere around here, and then a ton of grief and no real chance to ever even move up or anything. That's all you get for wrecking your damn life and marriage and sleep and whatever else.

It's not like they're gonna ever make me a detective or anything. Doesn't matter that Colin and I handle the most calls. Make the most real arrests. I mean we're not talking about garbage drug busts that any chump can make, the kind that gets you into narcotics. We don't make those. They don't matter. We make real arrests, for real crimes. For real assaults and robberies and murders. It was us that got that kid who offed his mother. It was us who got that hit guy who nailed the twin of the numbers' runner. No, we're not brilliant. We just work hard. The hit guy? Well, we talked to every damn person on the street, or near the street, and we came up with a plate number and a description and we got him. We got a "thanks" from the captain. Those two jerks in squad four, Marone and Alberts, those two jerks make a string of two-bit crack busts – busts that do nothing except get them off the street for the whole night and get them overtime – and they'll get transferred to Bronx Narcotics. They'll be gold shields in two years, making four grand more than we do. They get paid while we pay. I ain't crazy; I'm just pissed at everything. Got a right to be.

When did this start? On that night last November? God, it was so fucking cold. Rare in New York. Thanksgiving's always around 40 or 45 degrees in the rain. Know that weather real well. There was that one Turkey Bowl game I played in as a sophomore, New Rochelle High School against Iona Prep. My one year of attempting football. I was OK, and got to play because people were hurt, and so I was on TV, because that game's always on Channel 11 for some reason. It rained that day. Rained the other years when I just went to watch and get high and hang out, after switching to soccer as a fall sport, which is better for a midget like me. Even now, Colin and me are the "dwarf-mobile." No future in being a mediocre smurf halfback on a mediocre high school team. Nor in being a short, white basketball player with no jump. Or a lousy hitting catcher in baseball. All of which I was. And that was OK. I mean the game's the thing, right? For me the real opportunities lay in the warm water and muffled quiet of pools. Swim I could. Swim really fucking fast. Swim so well Michigan State University offered me that scholarship.

Now that was a cold place. So cold. Buried in snow for what, eight months, at least it seemed that way. The only place that was warm was the pool. The only place comfortable was the pool. The only place safe was the pool. Cold sucks. Cold is unsafe. Cold kills. I used to walk the streets in winter back in middle school, freezing my ass off in my denim jacket and b-ball shoes, looking in house windows, trying to see what normal families looked like. They looked warm. Cold sucks. But to hell with everybody. I've survived, even in the cold. I've been a college athlete. I'm alive. Who's done what I've done? Tell me that you've done what I've done and then talk to me.

That November night. Monday, Jesus, nothing's supposed to happen on a Monday night. That Monday night was just the day after Thanksgiving weekend, but it was Michigan cold. Freeze the homeless cold. Nasty wind shrieking right down from Montreal. Remember riding down to headquarters at the start of the tour right around midnight. On Police Plaza all these guys were crowded on the grates over the subway, grabbing whatever heat was filtering up. "What a fucking city," I said that to Colin. "What a *fucking* city." All these homeless right here between the Municipal Building, Police Headquarters, and the damn Federal Courthouse. On this big, fancy brick plaza, the Municipal Building lit up like a fucking wedding cake. Headquarters, oh, *I'm sorry*, "One Police Plaza," all glowingly high-tech. Right here, surrounded by all this, and they'll be lucky if they don't freeze to death before morning.

Other than that, we did nothing that night. Ate breakfast around four with Lieutenant Mack. Ate at Grucci's place just over the bridge. Old, kind of dirty, kind of like you see in those old movies with John Garfield or Bogie. But awesome food. Best breakfasts. Better than even the diners of New Rochelle, four more miles up US-1. And New Rochelle is where they make diners. Like almost invented diners. Serious. I even played Little League for the "Cassini Diners." We know diners. And diner food. Something like one diner per square mile. That and 7-up and cheap bandages. That's what New Rochelle does. Whatever. Anyway, I know diners, and Grucci's is not a diner. Wasn't built in a factory. Wasn't pulled here by a truck. But Grucci's had diner food, and diner hours, which is that you never, ever close. And so we liked it there, especially after midnight.

So we were there. Eating omelets. We talked about kids. Christopher must have been, what, 18 months I guess. Mack's youngest kid is about the same. Colin said he needed to talk about sex, not the after effects. But he's a minority now, at least among all of us who've got any time in. We've all got kids while he haunts the weird nightclubs in Manhattan – hunting. Or he wanders around shoe stores offering to buy women stiletto-heeled boots. Or, like whatever he does with his handcuffs. He never has those with him his first day back after days-off. So yeah, we talk about kids. Fact is, even the guys who are still married, who aren't the only parent, are usually the main parent. We're usually home all day, so that's what we do. All the guys who work steady midnights, Mack included, do the late tours so they can be home while their wives work all day. Yes, economic survival among New York's civil servants.

I'd guess we had two jobs the whole night. That was it. Maybe an accident and some stupid drunk arguing in a grocery. Nothing. Silent.

I was driving, like I am now, but at six I was fading fast, really crashing. We got the papers and coffee and were sitting there in the park trying to stay awake. Just out there along the river in Bronx Park. Don't usually go there, not usually our sector, or our river. Yeah, sometimes cause there's this Irish bakery nearby that makes the best scones. The best. Or to back-up other cars, or stuff. But usually we leave the Bronx River – this park, and all the damn tenements up to Electric Avenue, which is what everybody calls White Plains Road because the El is always sparking overhead, and all the tenements that go back down the other side of the hill – we leave all that to other people. I don't know, I just don't like it. Over here, you're always going up and down fire-escapes, jumping roof-to-roof, and running through these damn rat infested alleys. I don't like it. I mean, OK, our side, the shacks behind shacks – behind old little houses – with five families in each, and of course, the mother-fucking projects, and all the damn crack and weed dealers, that sucks too. But, I guess I know it better now. And this side, over here, this is junkie-land, and I don't like it.

So I can't really say why we're in the park. Why we're hiding here. You know, something about being in the wrong place.

So, we're just sitting in the wrong place. I'm reading about how the Jets suck in the *News*. Colin arguing out loud with the *Times* editorial page. Nothing.

Then, somehow over the heater and the radio, and through the window, I think I hear glass breaking. That should have been hard to hear. Should have been impossible. Shouldn't have heard it at all. Then it would've been nothing. Just a meaningless crime report for the day shift. A meaningless alarm. One more little crime in New York City. And my life might be completely different right now. Completely. Well, I don't know. Shit happens you know. Maybe if not that, something else.

Anyway, I shouldn't of heard it, but I did. I'm the good cop, remember. The good, dependable one. I rolled down the window, threw the car into drive, and spun around the wall we had parked behind, right out onto the street. Just in time to see this asshole tossing his bam-bam on the seat and starting the car. But not fast enough to stop him.

So we chase. Colin calls it in, and we chase. Up along the park. Across 233rd Street. From the place that looks like movies from The Bronx, els and tenements, across what might be some suburban "mile road" in the Midwest, and over to what could be the rubble of some New England port town gone very bad. Then up the Post Road and toward the "high bridge" that carries US-1 over the river here. Crazy. Fast. An hour later and I wouldn't do this. Let the asshole go, too much traffic, too many people. I'd've stopped.

But at six, its clear cold empty streets, and we're blasting across them. Someone, I know now it's Dan, but I didn't know it then, says he's ahead of us, up on the other side of the bridge. The stolen Firebird goes over the bridge and the perp sees the other radio car. He makes a fast left into the big old 1960s shopping center – dank gray concrete and cheesy aluminum – but he makes the wrong left. He hasn't hit the main lot, and we corner him behind Citibank, trapped at the drive-through so to speak. Those red lights over the lanes are for you bud.

Dan gets out of his car. Sue's his partner and she gets out to. The perp jumps out. Colin and me are sprinting, and man, it sure doesn't seem possible that we could be so far away, but everything happens before we get there.

The perp's six foot four maybe, huge. He spins and lunges at Sue, knocks her down, is taking her gun. It's that simple. I tell this story a million times to a million people. So does Dan, so does Sue, so does Colin. We all tell it, and every time we tell it we feel sure there should be more but there isn't. That's it. It's that simple. Sue rolls out from under him, but she's still reaching back for his hand and the gun, and I just blow the fucker away. I thought I emptied my gun, but I didn't. Four shots. Every one hitting him in the chest or side. Instantaneous they said. I got the heart. Pretty amazing for a guy who can never hit the bullseye at the range.

Four shots. Hot-loaded .38 rounds, nine-millimeter power, copper jacketed hollow points. Illegal ammunition, of course, though no one ever actually mentions that to me except one woman at the morgue, and I was certain – just something I knew – that she wouldn't put that in any report.

Dead. Dead, dead, dead. Michael Leroy Robinson. 17-years-old. Dead, dead, dead.

Of course, I was the only guy that fired. Colin didn't. Told me later that when my gun went off he kind of froze. Like a mini trance, he told me. He didn't tell any of the hundred or so damn investigators that. Neither did I. None of their business. Dan didn't either. Don't know why. We're not that kind of close that we'd get into that. Sue couldn't, though she was reaching for her second gun with one hand while fighting for her service revolver with the other. Told me later that the last person she wanted shooting at someone touching her was a guy who could barely qualify on the range. But that was long after she had said thanks in a bunch of different kind of embarrassed cop ways. And after we had had an awful lot to drink.

We all stood there. I don't know how long. Like I said, I can't figure out the time at all from the moment I bounced the car into park. We stood there. I remember the wind blowing and the red lights bouncing around the shopping center, but nothing else was moving. Nothing. Then Colin grabs his radio in his left hand, and sounding too calm – kind of robotic – says, "Central, Four-Seven-Adam, we got a perp down at the north end of the Post Road bridge. Behind Citibank. We need a bus and the Four-Seven supervisor." His right hand is still pointing his gun. My right hand does the same. So does Dan's. Sue has rolled away about three feet, and her gun is pointed too. I mean I guess Colin did that. I remember his gun being out. I remember the sounds. But I can't remember seeing him talk. Instead, I remember thinking, "Why do we call ambulances a "bus" anyway?"

Then the only sound is the wind off The Sound and the river flapping a torn flag. And for some amount of time – no one moves. Until Sue. Sue gets up real slowly and looks at Michael Leroy Robinson, and puts her hand on his neck artery, and stares. Kind of like when you kill a mouse, or even a bat that's in your house. Kind of like that. We had this bat in the house two years ago, just flying all around, and I couldn't get it to go outside. All I wanted was for it to go outside. Just like, I guess, all I wanted was to bust Michael Leroy Robinson for Grand Larceny Auto, a crime that doesn't even carry jail time in this city. Didn't want to hurt nobody, not the bat, not Michael Leroy Robinson, just get them to follow a couple of damn simple rules. Wild animals outside. Leave other people's damn cars alone. That's all. But I killed them both cause I couldn't do anything else. I killed the bat with a broom. Knocked it out with the broom part first, then smashed it with the handle. Dead. Stuck it in a big jar. I think a giant jar that had been for pickles or maybe peppers from the food warehouse. Whatever. Put it in the jar. Then Carolyn says, "Oh it's so cute." Which, of course, it was. Just a furry little flying mouse. Probably once pretty intelligent as rodents go. A good animal. Eats the damn mosquitoes. A cute animal. Big eyes, cartoon kind of face. Dead, it sure don't look like no big threat anymore.

And Michael Leroy Robinson suddenly looks thinner, less powerful, and much younger than just that moment before. The moment before he was the devil himself. Lucifer hurled at us in human form. Now he's a fucking kid. Just a fucking kid, with blood pouring out all over his Georgetown University jacket.

Still, no one's moving, except Sue, who gets up off the ground and comes over and pushes my arm down to my side. "Nice fuckin' shooting," she says. "Thanks." Nice fucking shooting? Whatever.

Off in the distance sirens are screaming and we see lights over on the other side of the bridge, red flashes sparking off the low clouds of dawn here by the swamp. That breaks the freeze frame, and Dan and Colin holster their weapons. Sue, being smarter than I could be in this situation, isn't sure what to do with hers. Fingerprints and shit. Fingerprints that will prove my story, I suppose, when the *New York Post* declares that I have killed some "honor student" in cold blood. She holds the gun lightly by the butt.

I'm just staring at this dead guy. Just staring. It's then I can first tell that this big chunk of me has vanished. Vanished. Just vanished. Maybe not as big a chunk as Goldstein. Goldstein was in my academy classes. We went drinking together on Fridays back then. But he got sent to another precinct. We didn't see each other much. Two years ago Goldstein, coming to the back of a liquor store on a robbery with shots fired, shoots a guy coming through a door at him with a gun. Unfortunately, it's the storeowner. Man oh man. Does not matter one bit to Goldstein that it's a "clean shoot," according to everybody. Doesn't matter that not even the papers make it a big deal. "White Jewish cop kills white Italian storekeeper in accident" just isn't inflammatory enough for New York's tabloids. Being totally justified doesn't matter. The lights go off in Goldstein's eyes. I see him a month later. He's still a zombie. Two years later, that hasn't changed. I think he works down at headquarters, maybe the property clerk's office, where maybe he feels he has no one to hurt. I don't know.

But what's my problem? This isn't just a "righteous" shoot; this is a damn heroic shoot. Eventually they will say that. The New York City Police Department will, in fact, just one month later, pull me downtown, pin this medal on me, and say I'm a hero. The union will give me an award. Young cops coming to the precinct from their rookie units will look at me with awe. The stupid ones hoping they get the chance to do what I did. Well, like I said, do the things I've done, and then come tell me about it. Just be there first folks. It's different on the other side.

The next night I dreamed "the dream" for the first time. Not that night, that is the night that followed that morning. That night I don't think I slept at all. Just tossed and turned. Walked out to the little gravel beach that is ours and kicked at the water, stared at the flashes of the Execution Rocks Light, tried to pace my breathing to the foghorn, and thought and thought. I learned long ago that if I could breath along with that foghorn, I could find peace in that, if only for moments. But the next night, so totally exhausted, the next night I fell asleep and dreamed the dream and woke up literally screaming.

Hey! Bad dreams don't mean you're crazy. I mean, I've had bad dreams all my life. Bad, bad dreams. And people have said I'm not crazy. Professionals have said I'm not crazy. Sometimes they look at me funny when I say stuff – like that department doctor did when I was getting interviewed for the job. At first I thought they talked to everyone, after we'd all taken all those unbelievable "personality profiles" that took hours and hours. But they didn't. Just some of us, including me, but including Colin also. And they hired both of us. It's just bad dreams. I'm not crazy.

But this dream is really, really bad. In this dream, I'm lying in a coffin. Yeah. Lying in a coffin. And I'm there because I'm dead. Yes, I'm dead. I know I'm dead, but even though my eyes are closed, I can see. Maybe you can do that when you're dead. Probably not. I don't really believe in heaven or hell or anything. I'm supposed to – I've been taught to since the very first. But still, I guess that when you're dead, you're dead. Maybe not. No way of really knowing.

Anyway – I'm dead and looking up out of an open coffin in a funeral home. I don't know which funeral home, but it's an old one. One of those giant old mansions converted into a home for the dead: columns, wildly decorated plaster ceilings, huge windows with heavy curtains. I guess it doesn't matter, but sometimes I think it's the one in Yonkers where my godfather's funeral was. Does that matter? No, I don't think so. It's just a funeral home. Big flowers on either side of the coffin, lots of chairs, lots of people. I know I'm in uniform. I can even see that weird green and white police department flag off to one side. I can see family around. I can see other cops. The cops are all in uniform, which is wrong if it's just a visitation or if it's a wake. But maybe it's right before the funeral. Then it's OK. Yeah, I'm enough of a romantic. If I die then bury me like a New York cop. Give me the honor guard, the white gloves, and all. Bring the piper to the cemetery. Play "Danny Boy" in that deep, mournful way up on a hill. I don't know what cemetery. Maybe where everyone is buried up in Westchester. It's on a hill overlooking the Taconic River valley, near the big dam, lots of huge trees. Seems like you need a hill so that the piper can be up there silhouetted against the sun, lonely, playing mournfully. Yeah, a hill is important.

But then Carolyn comes up to the coffin, and she's holding Christopher, and he's crying and yelling, "Daddy get up! Daddy get up!" And that's it. I wake up screaming.

The night of the day after Michael Leroy Robinson died I dreamed that. And I've dreamed it about every other night since. Though since Carolyn disappeared a month ago her face has gotten less and less distinct. I don't know. Maybe it was getting less distinct before too. She'd probably say so anyway. But I don't remember that. Last night I had the dream and the women holding Christopher might not even have been Carolyn, it might have been Maggie from high school. I don't know. It doesn't matter. It's just a repetitive dream. Not a guarantee of insanity.

Lieutenant Mack is the first guy to get there. Johnny Murphy's driving him. The ambulance gets there almost the same minute. So does a car from Pelham Manor, which starts at the city line just two blocks away. Then two more cars. I'm not sure of everybody who shows up, but Bobby Dixon's there. I remember him. Bobby walks right up to me, looks at the boss, and says, "He's going sick, get another bus here and get him to Jacobi." The paramedics just say, "D-O-A." They're bundling up Michael Leroy Robinson, whose name we now know because Johnny has pulled his wallet out of his pocket. They're bundling him up and loading him for that same ride to Jacobi.

Lieutenant Mack says, "Sure, yeah," and then to Johnny about getting my gun and bagging it and getting Sue's gun and bagging it. Then to me that I'm OK and to keep my mouth shut, and he'll be down at the hospital in no time, and to Colin to stay with me and Dan too and to Sue to also go sick right now and get to Jacobi. It's the procedure. It's the way it is in these stupid times. You can't say, "He was about to kill another cop so I shot him and that's that." You can't just tell the truth. The city is already preparing its case. In minutes, the *News* and the *Post* and *Newsday* will all be on the scene making their case. None of these will necessarily be my case. The union, my bosses, they'll be working on my case, and they want time. So Sue and I will go sick. We'll go to the hospital and be given something that is really just a legal recreational pharmaceutical as fast as possible, so that no one from downtown or Internal Affairs can talk to us until everybody has their story straight.

Bobby rides with us in the back of the bus. We go to Jacobi, the typical New York Municipal Hospital, where, yes, they're the absolute best on gunshots and knife wounds and burns, but come in for a gall bladder problem and they'll kill you sure as shit. We go there. They clear some space and we're just sitting in a corner. Some young intern takes our blood pressure. Bobby says give them Vicodin. I say, "Yeah, yeah, give me Vicodin," but he won't. He gives us Valium, which isn't enough, but I hassle him until he doubles the dose for Sue and triples it for me.

I just keep saying, "He was gonna kill us over a fuckin' stolen car? What the fuck?" I say that over and over until Bobby gets me up and pushes me to the phone on the wall. "Call your wife," he says. "No, I don't want to do that," I say. But Bobby knows the drill. He tells me I'll be late getting home, so I have to call. Then, if she turns on the radio or the TV she's gonna know about this instantly. "You want her to hear it from WINS?" he asks, "No you do not." So I call. Maybe it's a quarter to seven now. Maybe seven. I call. She's up. I say something, starting with, "I'm OK." That'll prove to be the biggest lie, but it has to be said. Then I trail off. Bobby grabs the phone and finishes the conversation. He does the same with Sue and her parents. Though she's a lot more coherent, Bobby still has to finish the call. This is another procedure, of course, though it isn't written down anywhere. If the cop, or the victim, or whoever can make the call, they make the call. Anyone who has ever made the call, or shown up at the door, for someone who can't, knows why.

Mack comes down and listens and says some stuff. I tell him I want my gun back and he tells me to stick with my off-duty gun for the next couple of days, since "you're taking them off anyway." He makes a bunch of notes. Tells me it's all fine. So does the union guy, so does the Chief of Bronx Detectives who's there, since I am sick, "just informally." He's also the father of one of my best buddies from the academy. He knows me. I'm not worried about him.

I go home. I drive from the station house back across 233rd Street. I go back over that bridge, and slide past that shopping center now swarming with TV crews. I turn right into the extravagance of Pelham Manor, a tiny island of wealth, and roll past the mansions till I hit the shore. Then, I swing back west along the Shore Road. I drive under a canopy of naked branches in Pelham Bay Park along the rocky shore. Then I turn left and cross the little drawbridge and I am back on the island, though it is not the refuge I had hoped. Past the tourist restaurants almost all shuttered this time of year, past the marinas and drydocks with the boats piled up. Just past Minneford, where the America's Cup yachts all used to come from when they were cool 12 meter yachts and not those stupid billion dollar things they race now. Minneford and the fishing boats are the heart of this island and this shore, and should hold at least the warm memory of hot summer days, but not this morning; it is still too cold. I go left again onto a tiny one-lane street and drive to the end, where a red light glows dimly for the road, backed by a green light that glows dimly towards the water. I crunch onto the ground shells of my driveway, climb out of the car, go up the porch stairs, and Carolyn, well Carolyn looks at me like I'm some kind of psycho mad dog. Really, like some kind of mad dog. I've seen it before. When shit goes wrong with cops anywhere. Like a shooting, or a beating, or some asshole ripping off drug dealers. If it makes the papers or the eleven o'clock news then it applies to every cop – every cop. I think about how, way back in the 60s, which I can't really remember except that I've seen it on TV, the soldiers would get off the damn planes in San Francisco, coming back from hell over there in Vietnam, and people would be screaming at them. They were coming home from an absolute hell that, of course, they never wanted to go to in the first place. And even if they did want to go, it was only out of whatever the fuck they thought patriotism was, or duty to country, or whatever. They'd get off those planes – finally coming home, finally safe – and protesters would be screaming through the chain link fence, "Babykillers!" Screaming that and meaning that – at guys who, Jesus Christ, at guys who just wanted to get the hell out of those damn uniforms and back to some kind of family or house or normal way to be. *"Babykillers."* Jesus Christ.

Now I really know. Because people look at cops the same way, every time something goes wrong. Every time. Doesn't even have to be a big wrong. Damn, I mean, I don't know of any cop-generated massacres anywhere. We don't burn villages, not even on our worst days. No we don't. But that doesn't matter. All that has to happen is that somebody's uncle gets a Goddamn ticket and pow we're all bad guys. Dangerous, crazy, bad guys. Someone dies and we're war criminals. It's not just cop-haters. Not by a long shot. It's everybody, right on up to the Goddamn mayor. It's everybody. Bankers and teachers and artists, mailmen and housewives, and the rich assholes down on Wall Street. And it's Carolyn too. Her too. Maybe she started out seeing me as a little, I don't know, heroic. That was as a jock. That was as a cop. Not the same as the self-absorbed wimps from the English Department she'd dated before. After all, I had the swimmers' body, toned and perfected and even, God help me, shaved. I thought differently. Talked a little less. Just did things. And the cop thing added romance and heroism to it all. It made the stories she'd tell her friends more exotic. More interesting than anybody she knew could match. But I guess she was never really sold on that. Few people are. Jocks are just eye-candy fantasy. Cops are just hired hands. Doing everybody's dirty work. Just like Vietnam grunts, or the poor Air Corps pilots and crews still blamed for Hiroshima and Dresden, as if they really had anything to do with it. Just babykillers. Now Carolyn sees me as that. Babykiller. Well, you want to hug a babykiller? You want to make dinner for a babykiller? You want to screw a babykiller? I didn't think so.

She goes to work. I bring Christopher to Mrs. Carramucci's across the street. She's the grandmother I never had. A safe place for him with soft worn furniture and the smell of baking. I lay down, but cannot sleep. When I get up and go out for a walk, Michael Leroy Robinson's mother is crying in a front-page picture in the *Post*. My name makes it to page one.

Jeez, it's three. Another hour to go on this tour-and-a-half. Put the car in drive, go around on up to the Post Road. Need coffee from the diner. Colin is totally asleep, snoring. Who cares. Nothing's going on. But at least two cars plus the boss are out at the house with arrests or that shooting. Means there may be just one other car and us out. Maybe there's another, or maybe they're out for "meal." I don't know.

You know, I hate all this "high sodium" lighting. I hate that night in the city is now pink. That every real color is twisted by the glow of that noxious gas. I'm not old. I'm not. But I'm old enough to remember incandescent streetlights. Spots of white light against the night. True night. Now even on the dopey little road I live on, with six houses, brick paving and nothing but an old abandoned ferry pier at the end, there are two, count 'em, two high sodium lights. Well, there were two. The one on the corner's still there but I shot out the other one near John and Barb's house. Yeah, I was drunk. I took out this old hunting rifle from my grandpa. Took it out, cursed city life and the twentieth century. Cursed Thomas Edison. And I shot it out. Pretty cool. It blew with some pyrotechnics, then sizzled and hissed, and went away. But it wasn't just me. Really, it wasn't just me. It was a community decision. We live on this damn tiny little island in Long Island Sound. This tiny little island. With just tiny little stores and only one main street. And dirt roads. With fishermen and boat builders. And between the thermonuclear glow of

Manhattan to the west, and the sky brightening lights of my old home-town just east, we need it dark here. We need real night. We need stars. We all agree. No one's reported it out, so it ain't been fixed, and we're at more than a year so far. At least almost everyone thought it was OK, except Carolyn who told me I was a psycho and got further away. Still a babykiller. Still, maybe more so. Now I'm shooting right at home. Still, I'm not a psycho. I just like night to be dark. Is that really strange? Night is supposed to be dark. It is.

But this night isn't dark. It's pink. And pinker still in the lot of the Baychester Diner. I get out. Say what I'm doing to Colin. He mumbles. I climb the stairs and walk in and go to the counter. It's way too bright in here. So bright I can barely see. Like looking up at the beach after you've fallen asleep. Everything is just way over-exposed. Just flashes of color in a sea of white light.

When I came back from Michigan, where "coffee" means coffee, I had to relearn this. Still, every time, which might be five times a day, I'm confused by it. Why is "regular coffee" coffee with milk and sugar in it in New York? Why do I have to say "coffee black, no sugar?" Why? I can't figure it out. Of course, just mine is that way. Colin's is just "black" which means that there's sugar in it. Still, it doesn't matter. He's not drinking it anyway. Just something I think about. I think about a lot of things. They're no big deal. No big deal at all.

I'm back in the car. Put the coffees down. Colin mumbles again. I cruise over to a dead-end by I-95 and the river. The Hutchinson River, drifting slowly through the cattails and other weeds here near the mouth. Stop. Stare. Nothing's going on. When are we off? Did he say four or four-thirty? Now I can't remember. Doesn't matter, we'll go back in at a quarter to four and see, or just split then. I guess it depends on the radio. Right now, it's silent. Silent.

I spent the week after Michael Leroy Robinson died doing nothing but talking to people about it. Sort of. I talk to my friends, my parents, my sister, other cops, the Internal Affairs guys, the union guys, the bosses, the detectives, the D.A.'s office. Not the papers. Not TV. I won't talk to them. I don't have to. Not to Carolyn either. She won't talk about it. She's got nothing to say to the babykiller in her house, and she slides so far to one side of the bed that I can sprawl now, like I used to before.

No, I guess she never really liked that I was a cop, anyway. Never did. I guess she was also always more political than I was. I mean, I'm a big left-wing type, at least in terms of social and economic justice, which is not as unusual as you might think among cops, at least the variety that work the ass-end of the world that are the bad areas of New York's outer boroughs. But I've got no problem with the flag, or hunting, or drinking at an American Legion. Maybe I'm a liberal and she's a leftist. Nah, that ain't right. I'm not sure of the words, but there was a difference. Anyway, I don't think she ever liked it. She did think I was heroic at first, at least a little bit. Maybe the uniform was even some kind of a turn on I guess. I don't know. But if either was true, it was against the major part of her nature. Against her grain. She was an English Department leftist. I was a dumb jock. Then I was a political oppressor. Only in the movies will good sex overcome a pile of shit like that.

Eventually, maybe in two days, we seem like we're speaking again. But we're not. We're just not silent to each other anymore. But speaking? No, we never do that again.

The press coverage dies out. Michael Leroy Robinson has a crying mother but not much else to redeem him, even in the *Post*. Eight burglary collars, three more for auto theft, expelled from school for carrying a gun. Not a nice guy. Won't play in the sympathy world. My name vanishes from the paper by Thursday. They keep me out sick for two weeks. I wander the malls with Christopher. Eat at Mickey D's a lot. Collect lots of Happy Meal toys. Or I sit home and watch old movies on cable. I swallow a lot of Valium. I dream the dream twelve times. Carolyn and I don't touch, even accidentally.

I'm clear. I return to the station house a hero. A big hero. I respond by hiding. I spend my meal hours downstairs in the gym, sometimes doing nothing but rowing on the machine for forty or fifty minutes, with the music cranked up. I stop showing up for roll call – I get to work late and dress while everyone's upstairs. Then I just walk out to the car. I spend twenty minutes in the shower after most tours, through the shift change, and all the conversations happen without me. If nothing else – I'm clean. Clean and clear.

Three weeks after that, sometime just after New Years, I beat the shit out of some dopey Jamaican who just has a big mouth. Handcuffed, I drag him up the stairs to the squad room by his heels. Then I go after him in the holding cell – Colin pulling me off and sending me out to get food. I don't even know what he said, but he pissed me off.

That's on day two of the week. I take the next three off, using up the tons of overtime turned into vacation time, but you know what? Time off ain't time off no more. At least not the same way. The off duty gun feels much heavier now. So I carry it less. I leave my shield, sometimes even my ID card at home. But I can't *not* be a cop now. Now I always am. Fucking Michael Leroy Robinson did that. He did that to me. Over a God damn stolen car.

OK, maybe I do get crazier. I start smoking more weed again. I've been pretty good for the years I've been a cop. Been pretty good. Now I've still got my rules; I'm gonna buy it. I will not take it off people on the street and keep it. That's not just illegal, that's unethical, and I won't do that. And I won't even buy it where I work. I buy it in my old hometown. That's OK. I worry about some random drug test, but I don't worry much. I can always make up the bullshit, talk about how much second-hand pot smoke we take in, in a precinct of Caribbean immigrants. And we always have Colin's example. When he was getting hired he had to borrow someone's urine to pass his physical.

Then I went back to doing coke with my friends from high school. And I start driving really fast. Even I know what I'm doing here. Yes, I know. But that makes the difference, right. If I was truly going nuts, I wouldn't see myself getting self-destructive. But I knew that's what was happening. And knowing it, I could keep it under control. I could.

I still go to work. Still do my job right. Still take care of my kid. I wanted to take care of my wife too, but there was nothing I was offering that she wanted. She worked longer all the time. Lots of late stuff. Mrs. Carramucci babysat a lot, even at night if I was working. Being a babykiller had pushed Carolyn not just away from me, but also out of the house. I should have cracked up then. I should have. In just a couple of months my life had gone from some kind of, I don't know, probably shallow but pleasant sit-com ideal to a total fucking nightmare. I should've cracked up then. I should have broke down then and just cried and cried till someone carried me away. But I didn't. Cause I'm not crazy. I kept doing my job, kept being a dad, kept cooking dinners. It might've been autopilot or something, but I kept functioning. Remember. I'm the guy you can depend on.

By the end of February Colin and me are doing coke in the radio car. Oh yeah, this makes sense.

In April, I throw some guy who's beating up his girlfriend down a flight of marble stairs. Luckily, he's real drunk and bounces real good. He breaks an arm, nothing else, and nobody says a thing.

In May we bust some asshole in a white BMW that's got 25 pounds of coke and thirteen stolen automatic weapons in his trunk. Best bust of the month. We get more medals.

That same week I realize that I haven't had sex in six months. No wonder I'm pissed, I think. But that fades. I don't really know anyone who'd screw me right now. Don't know anyone.

You know, I just don't know what Carolyn ever really thought of me. And that's after two years of dating and seven of being married. Maybe I was just good in bed. I guess I could take that. Maybe she saw me as a ticket out of her little town in Michigan. It sure wasn't like being a third-rate swim sprinter for a school, where no one watched swimming, carried any status. Besides, she was hardly the cheerleader type. She used to mock the team. Well, not really the team, really the whole sport. Or all sports. Or maybe everything I did. Ahh, cynicism and criticism, who wouldn't fall in love. But she was Midwestern pretty with hair that I adored. Hair that seemed like the froth of corn silk on top of oceans of corn. I thought she was brilliant, well, actually, she is brilliant in her academic way. And we drank in each other's bodies, inhaled our sexuality. And when I was inside her, or tracing my fingers along her body, or between her legs using my fingers and tongue to find the magical secret spots that would thrill her, or just curling up with her on those maniacally cold Michigan winter nights, then, I might, just...well, I might even relax some. Feel the muscles in my back edge away from the painful spring tightness that has ruled my life. That was addictive. Yes, that was addictive.

So we spent my whole senior year drinking and screwing and getting high and having her pick on me. What did I know? This was the first relationship since high school that lasted more than two or three months. And it was my senior year. Not that I was actually graduating or anything. I had nowhere near enough credits, but college for me was about four years of eligibility. So I was done. And like I said, I had become an addict. Maybe I made it more than it was. I probably made it more than it really was. People think women do that, but I think men do it more. Men are encoded with this need for romance, not women. Women have a genetic history that makes romance a path to what they need, which is keeping men around. Men stay because they need the romance itself. Anthropology and genetics according to me, OK?

Anyway, I was 22, and I wanted the American dream. Is that crazy? Probably, yeah. I should've gone back to New York, done whatever, fucked whoever, lived my life. Instead, I went back and took the police department test with visions of suburban split-levels and crowds of kids blocking my eyes.

Carolyn, of course, stayed for her senior year, coming to New York every holiday and lots of weekends. We'd walk Manhattan and she was enthralled. Could not get enough of it. Needed to be here. She made me love the city in new ways, just because she was so excited by it. I guess I loved her. I think I loved her. We had fun. I didn't want it to stop. I couldn't let it stop. So we said we'd get married, and we did.

It was sometimes good, sometimes OK, and only occasionally bad. We fought about kids some. I wanted more, faster, I'm not sure she wanted any at all. The first year we were married she had an abortion without telling me. That should have been it. Should have been. I'm Catholic for God's sake, even if I don't believe in anything the church says. Even if think abortion's OK for anyone else. It was inconceivable to me. Maybe I should've cried then and fallen apart – and gotten the hell out. But I didn't. I forgave. I accepted. I let it go. No, I guess I didn't let it go. I pretended to let it go. I wanted to let it go. Six months later we were back to what I thought was normal.

We fought about money more. She couldn't find a job that paid well in publishing, ended up working for New York Telephone, some kind of business account executive. She went from making nothing – and we fought about that – to making more than me and treating me like shit about it. But not often. Really, we seemed fine. We bought this ancient little house on City Island, and we worked on it. And she finally let herself get pregnant, and we had this cool kid. And she was, I think, surely at first, a good mother.

But I guess it wasn't what she came to New York for. Not to be a utility company drone living with a blue-collar cop on a street, in a place, that wasn't even as sophisticated as her little nothing hometown near Lake Michigan.

I guess when her blue-collar bore-her-to-death husband became a stone-cold killer it was the last straw. I guess. She never said.

It took seven months for her to fade completely out. I came home one day from a day-tour. The kind of tropical rainstorm that defines all of New York's seasons, flooding the island's streets, and pouring as if from a fire hose against the windows of the house that faced toward Long Island Sound. She was home, which was surprising. She hadn't been home any weekday before seven in months. But she was home. She said she'd been offered a transfer by the phone company. That she was getting a promotion in a Boston office. She was leaving right now. "Take care of Christopher." She walked out the door holding a big red umbrella, climbed into her Camry, and drove away. That was it. I sat down on the floor and cried. Right there by the door. Cried and cried not able to catch my breath. Then Christopher walked in from his bedroom. I guess I had assumed he wasn't there, was across the street or something. But here he was. I held onto him and he stared at me. Later we had dinner. Did I make it? No. We went to Mickey D's. Not that I can't or don't make dinner. I can, I have, I do. But that night I had to get out of the house, away from that place of dreams that didn't work.

Why'd I cry? For her? I don't think so. For me? Maybe. For Christopher? Yeah. For all my hopes and plans? I guess. You build a life on certain assumptions. Mine are gone. That's worth crying over, isn't it? That's worth freaking out over, isn't it? That'll make you crazy, right? Yes, it could. It would I guess. I don't know.

And if not for all that, then, maybe for that big chunk of me that got tossed in the gutter in that bank parking lot last year. Maybe I just finally cried for that.

Shit. What's that? Shit, "Colin, get up," I hit him and grab my radio. "Seven special five, central, whattayagot?"

Baychester at Two-Three-Three, shots fired, man with a gun, black male in an Orlando Magic jacket running east on Two-Three-Three. Possible man down in parking lot at corner."

Fuck. Fuck. Hit the lights, "Four central, we're two away." Hit the siren, the "Martian." No, switch to the "Nazi," the dah, dah "Hi-Lo," the soundtrack of all those European World War II movies. Scariest. Scariest. That's the idea here. You chase speeding cars with the classic American wail, run to medical cases and through heavy traffic with the Martian, but you scare people with Hitler's siren.

Central is asking for any available back-up. Is there any back-up? Silence, then, "Seven-Frank central, we're heading from the house right now, be there."

Colin's up, his gun is clear of his holster. We swing onto 233rd Street. Colin bangs his fist into his chest. "You and your fucking, 'I don't wanna change again' – crap. Where's my vest? Where's your vest? You go first."

I tell him to fuck it, don't worry, we're right there and nobody's there. No, I'm wrong, there he is. Not only there he fucking is, but I know him. We know him. Not only do we know him, we've popped him before – we've been looking for him for two weeks. Us and everybody else. When we busted him six months ago, he was just a low-level crack dealer. Nothing. Now he's gone big time. Seems like he's already shot a dozen people. Killed a dozen people. All dead from his Mac-10, the one that's in his damn hand right now.

He could turn and shoot, but he doesn't. He races for the door of one of the projects. I follow him, driving through a small chain fence, across a lawn, right to the door, just like TV, just like the movies. You just don't get many excuses to do this shit. You just don't. I'm doing it. "Stuntman," says Colin. Then, "He lives here, right? No, his aunt, his aunt lives here." "Yeah, second floor? Third floor?" "Second, maybe. Second, over there," kind of pointing at nothing.

We break from the car, run up the greasy steps, and in through the barely translucent doors. Fuck. I hate the projects. I hate the projects. It reeks in here. Urine, stale dope. Shit. It's dark, half the bulbs out. Cops die in the projects. They die in the projects all the time. We hear the back-ups coming, I scream, "We're going to two. You guys go up," to them, and we run the stairs.

Colin says, "That one," pointing at a door, but we bang on it and it's the wrong one. We know right away. Not sure how, we just know. But we also know we're close. We bang next door, some old woman answers. It's the aunt – we know it. We bust in, push past her, I don't think we knock her down, but honestly, who the fuck cares. Colin yells for the other guys, "Here, in here!"

This is always just like a TV show. So much like it, you start to think you're in one. Always bad. Need to stay real. If there is ever a time to stay real, this is it. Staying real keeps you alive. It does. It does.

Holding our guns in both hands, up and close, we slide, backs to the wall, around each corner. Want a fucking thrill ride? Try this shit. Try it on for size. This is not a Nintendo game. Game over is game over. I remember practicing this in the academy – in the "House of Horrors" at the range. They'd "kill" you seven, eight, nine times in an hour. I guess it had value. I guess you got some clue, but really no idea. No idea at all. You didn't want to fail there. Didn't want to embarrass yourself. Here, you'd take either of those things. You just don't want to die. Not this way, man. Not in this place.

Where is he man? Where is he? Maybe we're lucky, maybe he went back out the window. Maybe he just came in the building and went right back out. I'd take that now. Oh yeah, I'd take that.

The radio is saying something. I don't even know what it is. Can't know. But it's something about this. Later, man. Later.

OK, a bedroom. OK. But man, I'm tired. Man, I'm not up for this. I'm exhausted. What the fuck am I doing here? Shit. Wake up man. OK, a bedroom. I'm in – I kick the mattress off the bed. I kick the box spring. Nothing. Nothing. OK, the closet. I pull the door open and I see. Fuck! There's the gun – the barrel of the fucking gun at my head. OK, fine, fine, what the fuck anyway, fine. Time's up – right? The pain stops here. I hear a click. Christopher! Who is going to hold him there, seeing me dead? Who? But it's just a click, a wrong click. It's a fucking jam. A jam. I should shoot the motherfucker. I should shoot his ass dead.

But I don't. I don't know why. You know why? I don't know. Don't know. I reach instead with my left hand. I grab hair with more power than, well, with more than I've got. I start throwing the hair and all that is attached forward, onto the floor. While I do that, I crack the barrel of my gun across his head. Whack. Crash. He drops.

I stop. Still haven't said a word. Then I remember. I kick the gun out of his hand. Duh. Finally got around to that. Now what? Think, think, keep functioning. What? Oh yeah. "Got him!" I scream. "Got him, get in here." Amazingly, the room fills with cops instantly. Don't know where they came from.

I'm back at the house. Up in the squad room. Every fucking person there says either, "Great collar," or "Are you OK?" One or the other. A bust that clears now thirteen murders. One hell of a collar. The arrest of the month. Another medal. Once again the damn hero.

But also, I know what they're saying. "He's not all there." "Why didn't he shoot the guy?" "Because of what happened before, that's why." "And what was he doing, pulling shit like that alone, with no vest on?" "I'll tell you what, he's trying to kill himself, he's trying to kill himself."

I know. That's what all those, "Are you OK?" questions mean. They're looking at me like I'm pathetic or something. They're treating me like I'm something special. Special is bad. It means they doubt you. That's what it means. Somehow, sure it's my collar. Sure, it's my medal. But we'll get all the paperwork done. Don't worry. We'll take care of you.

No thanks man. That's what I need to say. No thanks man. I can take care of all this shit myself. I can. I can. But maybe I can't. I don't know. Whatever. I don't say it. I don't say nothing, except tell my story once. Colin types it up on one report. A detective, Erleich, he's doing it on all the other forms. Sure. I just cleared his damn board. Check off all those names. All those names.

I just sit. Just sit in the corner, lean back in the chair at someone's desk. Put my feet up. Start bumming cigarettes and smoking. I don't smoke. Except when I'm drunk, and now. Now I chain smoke. Lighting them off each other. Someone tosses a pack of Newport Lights at me. A whole pack. I just keep smoking.

Major case. Anyway, things are different. The bad guy has to stay here for a while, too many interviews. He'll be booked later. But I got to go down to the Courthouse and do the stuff with the D.A.'s office. It's after five. We go. Now Colin's driving. I'm just smoking.

The Bronx is still silent. But dawn is coming. We skip the expressways and head for the Concourse – The Bronx's ultimate boulevard, lined with the ghosts of the Art Deco wonderland that once was here – then we head down toward the stadium and the courthouses. Colin blows any light that threatens to stop us, but he does pull through a McDonald's for breakfast. Fine. It's free, but I'm not eating. Not now. I get more coffee, but it feels like it's chewing through my stomach.

My brain is sliding now. Sliding out of it. I don't know. The dream image is in my eye and I can't get rid of it. It's just there. Just there. Not exactly frozen, not exactly moving. Just there. All the time.

At the Courthouse we tell our story. Tell it to some asshole A.D.A. that I know is making more than me. Fuck him. Tell it simply. Explain where the prisoner is. Give him Erleich's name. Sign the forms. Bolt the building.

We stop on the way back. This time picking up a pint of Jack Daniels. I drain a third of it in one shot. It seems to do nothing. Colin takes a big hit, then I pour most of the rest down my throat. It doesn't change the pictures.

Don't have to change. Just sign out. The boss says take tomorrow off, go to court on this the next day. Doesn't matter. Fine. Whatever. Find my car. Someone asks if I'm all right. "I'm all right," I say. Then I repeat it, "I'm all right."

It's less than fifteen minutes home. Less than. I walk in the door. I guess the air smells of ocean salt and fish. I guess the rising tide is lapping against the shore in its steady heartbeat. I guess the sun is rising, spilling gold the length of the Sound, from Block Island to me. It would be that way. I don't notice but it is that way here, awesomely beautiful when you can look up. I swear to you it is. It's just that now I don't smell it, or hear it, or see it.

Call Mrs. Carramucci. Say I just got home, that it's been a bad night. Can she keep Christopher till like three or so today? Or I'll call. She, as she always does, says, "Certainly dear, no problem. Are you OK?"

Stand in the bedroom, looking out toward the water. Stand there. Turn the TV on. Don't know what channel. Doesn't matter. Pull my shirt off, rip the badge holder chain over my head, and throw my shield and all those colored pieces of metal on top of the dresser. Rip the ankle holster off. Drop my jeans and shorts, and throw my socks in the corner. Should put the gun away and take a shower. Should put the gun away and take a shower and go to fucking sleep. Should go to sleep.

But first, pull the gun from the holster on the bed and stare at it. Stand there naked in my bedroom by the window that looks across the Sound staring at this little five-shot Smith & Wesson. Stare at it.

Hold it so the barrel points into my mouth. Just hold it there. What would it be like? Not everybody gets to make dreams come true. Not everybody. Put some pressure on the trigger. Some pressure.

But no – not now. Not here. I ain't crazy. I'm not. Just had a bad month. A bad month. A bad year? Don't know. Take my finger off the trigger. Put the gun on the top closet shelf.

I should take a shower. I should go to sleep.

Run

Someone yells, "He's over there!" and you start to chase. On dark wet pavement through the thickest July-night air, you run down the block, through the alley, climb the rusty, shaky fire escape and there he is, just above, maybe two floors. Of course, he's in sweats and Nikes and you're wearing a fifteen-pound gun belt and a bulletproof vest that's choking your chest, and the black Adidas you're wearing are good, sure, but no match really. You're gasping for breath and shouting into the radio asking for help, even though you're not even sure what the address is, and he gets to the roof and when you get to the roof, he's gone. He might be running down the stairs inside, but you don't see him, or he may have jumped to that roof and be on those stairs, but your partner hasn't even caught up with you yet, so you can't search two stairwells. Most likely he's vanished into one of the apartments in the five floors below and he's hiding under a bed, or he went out and down a different fire escape – or the same one even – or he's catching his own breath on a couch watching Channel 11 with a quart of Miller High Life.

"We're on the block," you hear the radio say. "Where are you? What are you looking for?" "Male. Black," you answer, "Maybe six-one, about two hundred pounds, black sweats, black hoodie, white Nikes, Jordans I think." "What'd he do?" the radio asks. And you realize you have no fucking idea.

Centennial Park

I am sitting in the coffee shop because otherwise I would be sitting home alone, and I can't stand that anymore. Not that there isn't a lot I could be doing at home. I could clean up the damn kitchen, for example, or do the wash, or at least vacuum for God's sake. There's the Saturday night "premier" on HBO so that could be on in the background. But I need to be out, to at least see other people, and I haven't fallen far enough to be drinking again. So I am in the coffee shop, with my computer linked to their wi-fi, and thinking that if I would just start drinking again, and I was in the bar across the street, I'd find it much easier to talk to people. Alcohol does that in ways caffeine can never hope to.

Plus, if it was alcohol, I'd probably at least fall asleep tonight. Sleep has gotten really bad these days. It takes me hours of lying in bed, alternating between just lying there in the dark, watching TV, or trying to read. I see the clock count through the hours: midnight, one, two, three. Hopefully I don't see four, but drinking coffee now means I probably will tonight, but it's Saturday – tomorrow's Sunday – so it isn't really a problem.

It's not like I don't get tired. I do get tired. Just at the wrong time. At 5:30 I get home from work and I lie on the couch and I can't keep my eyes open. I'm exhausted. Making dinner, doing anything, seems impossible. I fight it, but the tired continues for an hour or two. Then, by bedtime, I'm awake. It's a cycle that desperately needs to be broken.

My father died in Florida. I think that was ten years ago now, though I can only figure that out by counting backwards from other events that are better marked in calendar years. I was not there when he died, although I knew then that I should have been, and know it even more now. But I was stuck in my own swirl of crises in Michigan and did not rush south when things suddenly turned bad and he was in the hospital. I let myself accept my mother's phrases that, "There's no reason to come now." I even accepted her thinking when I knew she was deciding whether to pull the plug, "It's my decision," she'd said, "There's nothing to talk about." I didn't get on a plane until after that Halloween night when my mother called – just as I was about to take my son out trick or treating – and told me he was dead. So I went to the funeral, which was possibly good for relatives and family friends, but had nothing to do with what I needed.

This afternoon I went to the art fair in the park downtown. I don't really like the typical art fair, because there is hardly any art, mostly dopey *Better Homes and Gardens* kinds of crafts, almost all predictable and hardly any creative, but I was at the library across the street and needed to be part of the community in some way, so I went. It is August and it is hot, and I stood in the lee of the fountain in the center of the park with the wind spraying me with an invisible mist of cool water, and I thought of other city parks, real city parks in real cities, on other hot days: Washington Square in Greenwich Village and Paley Park by Rockefeller Center and Buckingham Fountain in Grant Park on Chicago's lakefront. Central Park and Golden Gate Park and the Japanese Garden in the Brooklyn Botanic Garden. Places I could have been on this day had I made other choices.

I check my e-mail and find one from a high school friend who I have not seen or heard from in ten, no, more likely fifteen years – forever. He is in San Francisco and says that he put my name into a Google search and found sixty responses at least, including a short remembrance I have added to a New York Mets' history web site. He says he liked my little story of the first baseball game I ever saw. He asks what I'm doing and, "Where the hell are you?" He says he's a lawyer and that he has a two-year-old son and assumes, correctly, that my son is pretty much all grown up and done with high school.

I write him back, brief descriptions – where I am, what my job is (for that is pretty much what we mean when we ask, "What are you doing?"), and add a proud parent description of my child's success in high school. I wonder at the concept of me with a kid eighteen and him with a two-year-old. I say, "Write back, stay in touch."

Then I put his name into Google, but it is too generic, and returns two million, one hundred and thirty seven thousand, six hundred and eleven responses. Nothing in the first six pages is him. So I type in another name from high school and get fewer, but similar, results. I try another and may have found someone, but it is hard to tell. I consider e-mailing, but I'm not sure enough, and I hate to send, "Is this you?" kind of mail, so I file the link away and think that maybe I'll check it out later. On my fourth search, I do find someone. I even find a web-site promoting a CD he's put out with the remnants of a band that the site says was last together seventeen years ago, but I think it was longer. It was a pretty good band. They could get fifth or sixth billing at clubs like CBGB's in New York in the 80s. They had cool, memorable, I even thought sellable songs. Songs that should have caught on, but they got no breaks. I still have six copies of the one forty-five they made and a demo cassette I designed the cover for.

I think of other names but I go no further. I start thinking that this is too, what, weird? No, too depressing. Sitting by myself on a Saturday night cause I have no one to talk to, and trying to conjure up ghosts of friendships. Sitting in a tiny point of exile far out on the shores of Lake Michigan in the American heartland. Far from family, far from friends, far from my past. Succeeding? Well sure, in some ways. A new degree. A new career. Still in the people business but less violently, but, escape has its own costs.

My father was buried on a Thursday. Like today, it was hot. It was November but it was also Florida. I have always lived in the north and could barely understand that anywhere would be so hot at this point on the calendar. My son, who was eight, had gotten up at the funeral, unexpectedly, after I had read my eulogy. He had said that his grandpa had promised to help him build a treehouse this coming summer but now he couldn't do that. Everyone cried. Then I heard one old relative ask another, "Who does that blond kid belong to?"

At the art fair in the park there was a sketch artist doing portraits for fifteen dollars. I watched him draw what I guessed was a high school senior. He was not very good. I thought about a TV show on the BBC where a guy pretends to be a sketch artist, but the joke is that while the person is posing he's drawing something else entirely or just writing words. If that was going on here, it still wouldn't be original but at least I'd laugh.

The friend who e-mailed me was someone we picked on a lot. Once, in our school newspaper, someone wrote a restaurant review: "The burgers feature enormous onions," it said, "so those who tear easily, like…" and then it named this friend, "…who cried during *Love Story*, may want to skip the burgers and have something else." *Love Story* was our shorthand for the stupidest, sappiest crap in American culture. For those who don't remember, it is at least as bad a book as *Bridges of Madison County*, and a worse movie at that. Also, in the room that was designated as the "Library" of our alternative high school, but which was really just a place we smoked pot, there were no books at all except for sixteen copies of *Love Story* in French that sat on the one bookshelf.

Our high school newspaper often contained great writing like this. The story I remember best was about our basketball team during a season in which winning was, at best, a rare thing. The story started, "Twelve men walk from a cold night into an even colder arena. All know what they must do during the next two hours but eleven know they will not do it." Then it goes on to describe the supposed inner-mental-adolescent anguish of the twelfth, turning him into something like the strange descriptions of homeless people that fill *The New York Times'* "Neediest Cases Appeal" each Christmas – something else our school newspaper happily parodied. The story never mentioned the score or anything that happened during the game, which was unnecessary anyway. Considering this memory, I shrug off the depressive qualities of searching through my past and look up the twelfth player on Google and discover him to be a successful entrepreneur, an architectural historian who specializes in restoring ancient structures, and a part-time City College professor. He had grown up in an amazing historic house, one of the oldest around, from when people were really short. When you stood up your eyes were above the tops of most of the windows. We would steal those racist little jockey statues from people's lawns and leave them at his house. I'm not sure how his parents were selected for this particular on-going prank. Some-time, after high school, his parents split up. I think that one of them announced that they were gay, but by then I was out of touch and only know the story as rumor. I consider e-mailing him but put that on hold as well.

I had lunch at the art fair. At first, I thought the guy selling hot dogs from the pushcart was overcharging at two dollars, but then I realized that this is now the fare on the New York Subway. The friend who was in the band had a theory of economics way back then. He said that a Subway ride, a hot dog on the street, and a slice of pizza were always supposed to be the same price. He said you could tell if a fare increase was justified by comparing it to these two staples of the New York diet. So once I was comfortable with the price I bought a couple of dogs and a can of Coke and walked toward the gazebo to find a place to sit down and eat.

Children ran past me, playing tag. Just tag. Shouting and yelling in the sun. Their parents, nearby but otherwise occupied, only vaguely aware of where they are. This is accepted here. Of course it is. The scene is the myth. The sun. The green grass. The old Victorian houses that surround the park and form its unchanging backdrop. The Midwestern surety. That all adds up to a perception of safety, of kids protected, and allowed to be whole.

At the gazebo, I look back down. Hot dogs in hand. I see the scene, but I know other things. I know there are other things that run beneath this picture. I want it to be as it appears, but it is not. For among these children are the children who will later come to me. In the new job I have created for myself they will come.

They are from here, and yet they are children who are as I was. Mostly adolescent boys. The kind of adolescent boys who cannot quite look anyone in the eye. They sit in my office, disturbed by the slight flickering and humming of the fluorescent lights, and twist in their chairs, and sometimes they are so uncomfortable that we need to grab drinks from the machine and go outside onto the grass and walk as we talk. As we walk, I listen to their stories, stories that only bleed out of them under the exact right pressure of questioning. And their stories are of failure and violence and the need to hide who they are, and they have mostly given up, as their schools – parents – friends have told them to do. And it is my job to show them that there just might be a way out.

"It is funny," a woman who may soon come into my life has said to me, "that you can see the potential so clearly in these boys and you think so little of yourself." "I'm being punished for my crimes," I told her, feigning a laugh. "I have been all my life." But she does not laugh with me. "Get over it," she says. "Whatever you did you did because you had to. There's nothing wrong in that." On nights like this, I must work to even begin to believe her.

The gazebo is raised almost a full story above the park. It is really a very big structure, designed to be a stage for summer band concerts, and so below me, as I eat, the art fair and this summer afternoon spread out, like early in a movie and we are setting the scene. The children run through this cinematic frame and laugh and shout as the crowd swirls along the curving paths. The breeze ruffles the edges of the tents that house the exhibitors. There are occasional dogs moving here and there, and more kids, all kinds of kids, playing by the fishpond. Summer. America. The Midwest. The present day.

I watch, and I am here, but I also know that I could be seeing a different film. Standing in a different afternoon as a different scene unfolds. And I consider some other places that might be home.

I've always thought that if money just fell into my hands, and I could go somewhere and not worry about earning anything, than I would find my way to one of North America's secret places – like living east of Québec City along the Riviere St. Laurent, or in one of the once-were-resort-towns in the mountains of upstate New York or in Maine – as long as it was very far from where the people from Connecticut and Massachusetts live. I used to include places like islands at the north of Puget Sound or the Outer Banks of the Carolinas as possibilities, but I do not think they are very secret anymore and in the fantasy I absolutely do not want to live in a *theme park* of a small town, I want to live in a small town.

The other possibility, if money was no object, would be to go "back home," that is to New York, to New Rochelle or City Island or Brooklyn and live in the kind of places I have never been able to live in. A triumphal return that would shatter the limited expectations I aroused growing up.

In recent months, I have found myself daydreaming about moving to these places – even daydreaming them with this woman I might let into my life. But in order to do any of that, I need to stop being afraid of my dreams.

My dad was a hero in many ways. And I have always known that there was no way to match up my accomplishments with the life he led. Oh sure, I know his failings. Of course I do. I know the alcoholism and the violence and the fear, and I know the disappointments. But you can't measure a life that way, can you? He commanded a tank in Korea as a nineteen-year-old, fighting his way the length of the peninsula. Won the Silver Star. Was in the worst battles in the worst winters of that strange conflict. Saw, yes, inconceivable things that I now want to say, explained many later actions. This was all, of course, long before I was born.

But there is much more. Obviously, he was a dazzling athlete, a professional and a star even if he never reached the top. I think now of all the NHL hockey teams that fill arenas across the US and Canada, but back in his day that top rank was just six teams with small rosters. It was the tiniest fraternity – just a hundred and twenty players in all – and there was no shame in never having made that final step. But he was magical in any sport he tried. He could just do it. Without seeming effort or learning: baseball and soccer, throwing a football, picking up a hurling or lacrosse stick. He was like those musicians who hear an instrument and then can just play it. He constantly astonished me.

And he could figure out anything, and fix anything he bothered to try. He could build a house and rebuild a car engine and do plumbing and wiring, and fix any appliance that broke. But still those are all details.

He was depended on by neighbors, by cousins, by his friends. People would call, in the middle of the night, they would call: their cars had broken down, their dates were drunk, they were stuck here or there for this reason or that, someone was sick, someone had died. They would call and he would get up and go to them and fix their car or at least push it back home, or get them back to their houses and threaten their drunken companions, or solve their crisis or deal with the cops, the hospital, the undertaker. He would do all that for them.

I am not like that. I try. I really do. But I have never built those kinds of relationships, and my learning curve is always much steeper. Oh sure, I could swim. I really could. And I could hang around in a few other games. I was a good cop. Truly. Disturbed and all, I was still the kind of guy the bosses called when they needed things done. But that's not quite the same. And now, I try. I really do. I have worked hard to learn what I know. It has been a battle to discover the possible combinations of things that might allow a kid, a kid like the kid that I once was, to have a better chance. It took unbelievable hours of research and effort, and all the battles with all the things I have struggled with since way back when. And it makes a difference. It really does make a difference, when I break through a boy's fears and the schools' resistance, and the overprotect-iveness of adults. If I can break through those walls and hand a boy the computer or the software, or the thing that makes reading or writing possible or focusing on work possible, then I change lives. And that should be its own reward, I know, but it comes with no residual positives, without cheers, and with little money. And I go home to an empty house, unless the child has decided to stay in, because my own fears have left the walls too high.

I can't imagine my father on his deathbed. It is struggle enough to remember, for I have chosen to forget, worked hard to forget, how he looked in those weeks after his first heart attack and his bypass surgery. I sat down on the kitchen floor after my mother had called and said he was gone. My son, who was eight, had on a dragon costume made by a neighbor who just wanted to help because we were having such a hard time. She just wanted to help, it was a great costume, a spectacular costume, and Halloween was so important. It was the major holiday in my father's year. We would have pumpkin carving parties and create amazing jack-o-lanterns, and this was long before stencils and fancy pumpkin knives. His favorite holiday. Our family holiday. And I sat on the floor and held my son and told him his grandfather was dead, and he cried and cried, and I cried and cried, there on the floor. And then I decided that it would be unforgivable to not celebrate my dad's favorite holiday, but I could not just send my son, whose grandfather was just now dead, out trick-or-treating with the neighborhood dads and not me also, and I could not just lock the door and turn out the lights and not hand out candy either for this holiday demands both. So I had to call other neighbors and explain all this and thus elicit deepest sympathies, and get one or the other of those adults to come to our house and give out candy so I could walk with my son, and we could celebrate my dad's favorite holiday. And they came and I lit all of our pumpkins. Pumpkins with arched-back cats shining in their eyes and pumpkins in the middle of grotesque winks, and pumpkins with frightening faces of all kinds — the lessons of a childhood now appearing richer than it ever could have while I lived it, and we went out.

In Florida, they were taking my father from the hospital room to the morgue. They were tagging his body. They were putting him on a stainless steel shelf in a stainless steel refrigerator. I know all this simply because I have seen too much death, not because I have heard. My son and I walked the neighborhood, he running door-to-door, me strolling along the middle of the street, flashlight in hand, sharing small chunks of the thoughts racing through my mind with neighbors I did not have enough history with. A wake of strangers. It would be forty-eight hours before we got to Florida, to the funeral, to the relatives. And by then he was only history.

I could make other choices, I tell myself now. I could, and perhaps I still can. Christopher will go to college in the fall. He will move to the university. It will be only a couple of hours away but he will not be home. And after that, he will go further. He knows his history as a native New Yorker and he chafes under the constrictions of life in a small town. I have often thought that I needed to stay alive this long. This was the deal. I'd get him to adulthood and then I could go. This seemed both fair and reasonable. I'd take him this far and then I could find the peace of the full escape. After all, while we haven't had money, and we haven't had much, we've always had enough. I've done what I had to. Dinners every night and breakfasts every morning and always a roof to sleep under and a TV to watch *The Simpsons* on. And clothes and the instruments he needed to play the music that delights him. I got him to school and coached his sports teams and held him when he cried. The only parent since way back when. I've been there. Now he heads out into the world and – well – what about me?

I pack up my computer and leave the coffee shop. It is late and everything has shut down for the night. I dump my backpack in my car and walk along the dark streets, surprising myself when I reach Centennial Park again. The overachieving parks department has done a thorough job. Except for the bagged trash, there is no evidence of the day's events.

I stand by the fountain that babbles, the only consistent sound, and I wonder. I wonder what else I might do. I feel like I have fought so many fights, and have lost so many. I feel beaten and beaten again. But I will not, on this night, discount the victories. There have been a few. And now I lie down in the damp grass. I lie near the fountain and look up between the enormous old trees. I consider that I might try a few more things, or just try the same things again. I know the costs of defeat. I sure do. But I can also imagine the possibility of the taste of victory now and then. Somewhere in the back of my mind is the vaguest thought that there are things I could do which might change tiny parts of the world for the better. Even a shudder of recognition that I might have done so once or twice before. Just maybe. I am not sure of that. Not even close to sure. Out there also – I let myself think this too – out there across this small town, on this dark night, is a woman who might love me and accept me. And out there are those boys. If not someone like me, then who will they possibly have? In this lonely moment, I decide that I need not rule the possibilities out.

Lying on the grass by the fountain, I close my eyes for a full minute, falling into the deep. And then I open them and I look up at the sky, starting from Polaris at the top and trailing down to Orion, who lounges on his side to the southwest.

I remember being ten during the great Northeastern blackout of 1965. In that dark a family that often struggled, seemed unusually calm and OK, and at some point in the evening, I ended up on the roof with my dad, looking at the lights of heaven that poured above us, stunningly visible with the competition from earthly lights extinguished. My dad told me that when I was looking at stars I was looking back in time. "Like the Twilight Zone?" I asked. "Like when you go back and can make something you did wrong right?" He laughed and said, "Kind of like that." And we were silent for a long time. Later I overheard, as he whispered to himself, "Sometimes I wish."

Fifth Hour

Eighth grade Social Studies and I sat smoking a cigarette, my left arm outside the window between drags. Denny, sitting next to me, watched and got jealous. Pulled out his own, tapped one out, asked for a light.

At that point in adolescence, one bad idea deserves another, so I handed him my smoke so he could light his without the sulfur smell give-away of a match. Billy and Mark, fellow residents of the back of the room, shook their heads. Two rows ahead Susie Calabrese turned and mouthed, "You assholes. Gonna get busted," singing it without sound.

This wasn't the worst class. Hardly. But it was just after lunch, the afternoon sun was pouring through huge dusty windows making the room too warm, and Mr. Johnston was, if cool and unobservant, pretty boring, and you had to do something.

Denny exhaled, a plume of smoke curling upwards. The principal walked in, the heavy lacquered door banging behind him. My cigarette slipped from my fingers, dropping past Mr. Clark's shop class below. Denny tossed his into the book tray under my desk. The principal was saying something. Complaining. The old papers in the tray, tossed notes, messed-up assignments, caught fire.

It was quick. Denny reached with his arm, sweeping the papers out, burning himself, yelling, "Shit!" The principal stopped, stared. I stamped out the flames.

We got three-day suspensions. Perfect early spring days. We smoked Newports and drank beers sitting on a dock – our Chuck Taylors dangling above the water.

acknowledgements

It took more than seven years to write this book. Not working continuously, but seven years. Over those years many people helped by reading, by making suggestions, by encouraging, by saying, "You need to get this story published." To all of you – many, many, thanks.

There were some who did much more – whose encouragement and effort were given so generously – critical reading, editing, fighting with me over structure and words and paragraphs. Rhoda Janzen, Julie Kipp, and Chuck Warren all devoted hours to this book, and to them I am deeply appreciative.

And, of course, without my family, who taught me how to truly see, hear, and feel this world, I could not have even begun.

But without Jill Piers there would be no book. Not just her efforts – in reading and re-reading, editing and re-editing – but her boundless love and support of this work and the other pursuits in my life, made an elusive dream become a reality. Jill, with all of my heart – thank you.